DECEPTION

Part 4

Affairs of the Heart Series ~ Hollywood

KEW TOWNSEND

Tremmelle Publishing

HOLLYWOOD, CALIFORNIA

DISCLAIMER: *DECEPTION* is **Part 4** in the *Affairs of the Heart Series-Hollywood.* It is a strong "adult" themed work of fiction. This book is not for readers under the age of 18 or has difficulty with CLIFFHANGER ENDINGS. This title previously published as *Blood of the Hurri-Kaine.*

Publishers Note: Names, characters, places, and incidents are products of the author's imagination and are used fictitiously. Any resemblance to actual events, locales, or persons, living or dead, is entirely coincidental.

Author acknowledges the copyright or trademarked status and trademark owners of the following wordmark mention in this work of fiction — Hard Rock Café — All chapter headings using song titles and the musician names associated with them.

© 2016 Tremmelle Publishing, United States
© 2015 Cover Design by Sparkle Graphics
© 2015 Cover Layout by Jesse Kimmel-Freeman
© 2015 Cover images by Sergil Shalimor; Francis Gonzalez
© 2014 Book Layout BookDesignTemplates.com

Sign up for NEWSLETTER at www.kewtownsend.com

DECEPTION/ KEW Townsend
ISBN 978–06926474-2-4

Dedication

To my maternal grandfather Edward (Eddie) West. My love and affection to him for shaping my early musical influences and placing my feet firmly on the road to music. Grandfather Eddie played the Hawaiian guitar though I was introduced to it through Country – Western music, as it was known, a long time ago. As a child, I remember wandering around his music room that displayed guitars on all the walls. Below were shelves taller than I stuffed with crumbled sheets of music, and alongside the wall a stand-up piano, accordion, and an odd assortment of percussion instruments. His band, the *Eddie West Quartet* was well known in Hollywood during the 1920s and played all the hot spots and A-list parties. Family legend has him and Rickenbacker creating the first electric guitar.

CONTENTS

Chapter One

SEND HER MY LOVE

December 30, 1989

New Rochelle Hotel
Pasadena, California

ill death do us part.
It sounded long and permanent.
Holly Hill gave Luka Hunter what he needed of her kisses until the early darkness captured the last of the afternoon. How many times did she believe each kiss, and being in his arms, were the last?

When would they end?

Luka was agitated, and her kisses seemed to help him forget the menacing storm that raged outside her door, tearing limbs from long rooted trees.

The gale force wind blew strong it snapped signpost and streetlights like toothpicks while the muddy earth flooded the streets stopping the flow of life in Laurel Canyon.

Kaine Walker, moving closer and closer to the moment.

Outside was ominously dark. The gray light of day faded into the darkest of nights when evil took to the streets hiding in the black shadows.

The lightning claimed exclusive rights to hover over Holly's cozy home. And oh, how the thunder rolled. And in between the flashes, she looked to Luka — her rescuer and her lover, gazing into his strong, confident, blue eyes knowing he would never become her husband or her future. But she felt assured that her performance as a seductive concubine, these past few days, did convince him that she would stay with him.

For the present, everyone concerned was safe. Apparently, his pain and insecurities melted away. She caressed his soft beard and occasionally kissed his succulent lips, while she rested in his arms, contemplating the destructive forces closing in on her.

Her days with Luka revealed a surprising turn. He'd seen to her every need and enjoyed her reign as queen in Luka's world of airplanes, backstage concerts, executive homes, filming her TV show, and hanging out with movie and rock stars. No surprise, he'd been a remarkably brilliant and attentive lover. All because he'd taken a chance on her, opened his heart to trust her because he loved her too.

Luka made the task to fool him that she was staying, more of a pleasure, then the duplicitous truth that she'd been whoring herself out to protect her budding family. She found the sweetness of him like finding a diamond in the rough. He shared his hopes and dreams that defined him, with her and they became heartbreaking. But nothing changed the fact he was a dangerous manipulator, never to be trusted with her most precious gift. He'd made a mistake, a costly one. The master of manipulation and disguises let his guard down with her, became vulnerable, and made errors.

One extremely important slip-up cost him everything with her. And she remembered his words.

It's fitting I watch his child growing inside you and then assume the role of father. His child will be enough of a constant reminder.

There were too many warning alarms going off when he'd said 'constant reminder.' She lay there wondering what he'd meant but decided never to find out. The thunder rolled and shook the cozy nest again where Luka called home. And though she'd reminded herself of his chilling words, it was more difficult than she would have expected to leave the temporary safety and comfort of Luka's familiar embrace. And a bit more sentimental than she would have ever predicted, hoping her future would turn out as expected, this would be the last time he ever held her in his arms.

They were due at the New Rochelle, an old, nineteen twenties style aristocratic hotel that sat atop a hill on the outskirts of Pasadena. Solange and Ian booked the entire top floor for the wedding party. And since Holly and Luka were both in the wedding party, were expected to attend the wedding rehearsal set for a few hours.

As best man, so would Kaine.

All attendees were booked to stay two nights. That night for the rehearsal and then tomorrow for the wedding ceremony and reception — New Year's Eve.

"It always seems as if I'm packing. I hardly know where I am anymore." She bemoaned with a sigh.

Luka smiled. "See why I'm glad to have touring behind me?"

Holly quickly packed her outfits handpicked by Luka for the next few days. He'd taught her first impressions were important and reminded that she would mingle with the crème of the crop of possible guests for her show. She understood her place as the woman on Luka Hunter's arm — expected to be stunning. Especially for one important guest.

Kaine.

Luka spoke angrily to someone on the phone with his back to her.

Holly welcomed the distraction. She quickly packed Kaine's last gift to her in London, the beaded white wedding nightgown, and his recent unopened Christmas gift, to return in case their reunion didn't go as planned. Holly stacked her luggage by the door and stuffed Kaine's large gift box into an Asset boutique bag. Then she joined Luka in the bathroom brushing his teeth. She made it obvious that she took headache medicine, alerting him of the turns in events.

Now, he was like her in London. He never suspected a thing.

How well the master taught her.

Holly dressed quickly and soon they headed for the Dream compound, where he quickly repacked, and changed his clothes. Soon, they headed east for South Pasadena, where The New Rochelle Hotel stood with grace and elegance. A stunning, Art Nouveau monument high up on a hill, represented the early glamor years of Hollywood. The uniformed attendant took their luggage.

Holly entered the doorway and walked across the foyer. Her thoughts consumed her — *HE'S HERE!*

The bellman escorted them quickly up the exclusive elevator that traveled to the top floor and then down the long corridor to their separate suites. Holly's was located next to Luka's at the same end of the hallway. When she discovered that the rooms were adjoining rooms, she wondered why Solange placed her near Luka since she'd never approved of her relationship with him.

There it was again. Solange knew everything since the day she saw Luka kissing her backstage at Wembley Stadium in London. How obvious to Solange the existence of a strong relationship between her and Luka.

Perhaps she'd weakened.

She doubted it.

Holly's loved the outstanding three-room suite, decorated with an extensive collection of antiques, tapestries, and period furniture. She'd enjoyed this type of hotel grandeur and extravagance with Kaine in his penthouse in London. After she unpacked and surveyed the luxurious main room and then the majestic bedroom, she wandered into the adjoining spa/bath to Luka's accommodations and peeked in to look. His décor mirrored hers, and she watched him talking on the cellular phone. He was probably getting the film rights to the wedding if she knew him that is if he didn't already have them. She laughed at his resourcefulness.

His face shined bright and happy because he was doing what he loved most, next to her and waved her in as he finished. He moved close to her, close, oh so close, and kissed her, long and slow until the burn flared deep.

"Luka, my beautiful angel, I can't. To touch you makes me want you. And I'm exhausted from the *Bon Jour* junket and making love, and with the baby and all this excitement. We're expected at eight-thirty for the evening rehearsal and dinner and need to catch a quick nap."

Luka kept her in his arms. His intense gaze dove deep into her eyes as she tried to resist the stirrings.

"I see I'm going to have to put you on a diet of my loving straightaway," he declared and smiled that killer Luka smile of his that lit up a room.

"You're a mother after all. We need to make time for you to get your proper lie-downs and to eat well. Nothing can go wrong with this pregnancy or with you.

"I'll tell you what, so you can rest peacefully. Why don't you have a lie down in your suite? It will be quieter, especially since I have many calls to return and possibly a meeting or two. Then I'll come and wake you up in time to change clothes for the rehearsal."

Holly tiptoed up and quickly kissed his succulent, rosy lips, pink from her constant flow of kisses. She moved to walk away.

But Luka had a difficult time letting her go.

It was clear.

Kaine was there.

This moment with Luka different, quiet and assured, unlike her love with Kaine, dramatic and tempestuous. Later, she tossed and turned, surprised sleep avoided her especially being exhausted. There was one thing on her mind.

Kaine, any moment!

The thunder and lightning crashed relentlessly, pounding at her windows. She felt a bit sorry for all the wedding guests that traveled from around the world for these high-profile nuptials, in such abysmal and devastating weather, unlike California. As the lightning moved closer, it unnerved her.

She wondered where Kaine was. And a bit too nervous to sleep, she got up and wandered over to the large, gold box in the boutique bag that patiently waited for her attention. She'd wanted to open the gift from the moment it arrived.

She slipped out the small card, closed her eyes and took a deep breath, then opened them to read.

> **For My Lady Love,**
> **Sending you all my love,**
> **The keeper of my heart,**
> **To keep you warm, until I can,**
> **I'm on my way to you,**
> **I love you.**
> **Three times, four times, a million times,**
> **We'll always have the forever love,**
> **Merry Christmas,**
> **Yours always,**
> **Lancelot de *Hurrikaine*.**

Kaine's sweet, loving words targeted her hungry heart.

All the while, the thunder shook the building, intruding into her suite, jarring the wind temporarily from her. The emotionally charged words shoved her down onto the bed next to the box and paused, afraid to open it.

Holly hesitated, and then delicately pulled on the lid. Compelled to lift it quickly, like ripping off an adhesive bandage and peeked inside. Her eyes widened. A silky dark blue, fur coat. She yanked the soft coat from the box. It was light and tumbled to the floor. Three-quarters in length, it was a rich, elegant sable. The Asset label in the collar told Holly it was synthetic. These last few months' Asset advertised they ceased making any products with animal fur or skins after becoming active in preserving animal rights.

Holly ran her hand over the beautiful, lustrous, sparkling fur, slipped her arms into the sleeves and the silk liner glided along her flesh, cool and smooth to the touch. She pulled the incredibly beautiful glistening faux fur coat to close it around her as if it was Kaine's arms drawing her into the sacred circle of his love.

I'm on my way to you — I love you.

She fell into the magic memory of their first kiss during the music video at the Hard Rock, in London long ago.

Her magnificent Kaine loved her and expected to take her with him.

Chapter Two

I'M ON TO YOU

Kaine's expected arrival time — two hours for the rehearsal dinner. He would be there.

He was here.

In which room?

How close was she to him?

Her magnificent Kaine.

Holly imagined the faintest hint of his cologne lightly floating from the coat, and she fell into a rich, sensual fantasy. She imagined Kaine clearly, remembering his electric touch, his exquisite face, his piercing blue eyes, his one of a kind heart filled with passionate love.

Dizzy from his latest act of reminding her of his forever love, served to excite Holly. She took off his present, laid the coat on her bed like a precious gem. Hot tears burst into her eyes then flowed freely down her cheeks as she cursed him for his timing.

"Why the hell didn't you come for me sooner?"

Holly knew why. He was in the castle. She sobbed, drifting off into a dream state searching for her dream lover.

She waited for him to come to her side and comfort her. She saw Kaine kneeling at her bedside. His eyes burning with love, whispering.

"I'm on my way...."

Holly awoke with a start.

"I'm here waiting!" She said aloud. Then realized she'd dozed off, and his sweet face a dream to evaporate.

Holly rose, sleepy and groggy and wandered into Luka's room needing to retrieve a misplaced KeepAll. Instead, she found an opened box on his desk with a camcorder. She turned it on to say something to Solange and Ian about their wedding.

Noise at the door alerted her of Luka's unexpected arrived. Wanting to brush her teeth and hair after her nap, she ducked into the adjoining bathroom inadvertently leaving the camcorder running. She barely shut the door when a second voice arrived.

She remembered he expected meetings.

The voices were loud, growing louder. A flash of lightning cut through the night and filled her suite with the crackling sound. Frighten, she moved to turn away when she became acutely aware of Luka's anger.

Who was Luka angry?

Whom did the other voice belong?

A bit disoriented, she leaned against the thin partition separating their suites. Luka yelled at the other person. The heated conversation continued, and she wished the other party would speak up louder.

Luka's tone of voice blasted loud, harsh, but mostly threatening as he pointed out.

"I told Michael to extend the Bon Jour trip, and he did. I

needed to keep her away from that asshole in case he was keen on coming for her bloody earlier than expected. I can't trust that fucking sod."

What did he mean 'extend' the Bon Jour trip? Luka deliberately kept her out on the road with him and away from Kaine.

Why didn't that surprise her?

But to whom was he talking? They responded with something she couldn't hear. But Luka didn't buy it.

"It wasn't that grim in London, Sarah."

Sarah? What the fuck was that bitch doing here? Especially today?

Holly leaned up against the bathroom divider to listen to Sarah's thick, coarse, English accent.

"It was easier for you. You had the Princess Bitch to wine, dine and boff. I had a broken-hearted and violent Kaine to cope with day after day."

"Rubbish Sarah, you were well paid. You're on Kaine's payroll, and for the time being, secretly on mine. And I've paid you more than enough for your covert part."

"Not enough. I filled Kaine's bleedin' head with lies about her cock teasing all those rockers at Friar Manor. I fuckin' thought he would tear my bloody head off before he went after the skank. Your part was easy, take her aside and make it look like you had it off with her in the shadows. Kaine was outraged, went bloody mental! Worst I've seen in years. I was afraid he would have a go and damage or destroy someone other than her."

Luka grunted in agreement, "I have to admit, I was pleased to see how easy it was to wind up Kaine. I kept that pompous asshole coked up he didn't know which end was up for days. But I'm angry with you because you badly wounded Holly. You'll pay for kicking her."

"You said to scare her off for good with Kaine's gun, and I did. Put the bloody thing right next to her fucking head, I did. I wished it had loaded. Told her next time it would. You should have seen her face with her nose so high that I fucking kept kicking her. It was one of my better ideas that I should get rough with the Princess Bitch. Why are you puttin' on gloves?"

Holly listened to the sound of something hitting flesh.

"Rough. You mean like that?"

The sound of something smashing flesh happened again simultaneously as Sarah cried out in pain.

"Luka ... please ... don't. She's a tosser. That skank deserved everything she got and more. She's a nutter, believing she was Kaine's woman and not a stupid publicity stunt. Well, she'd another think coming. What is it about the slag, anyway? Does she have a golden twat?"

Holly listened on in horror, riveted, this must be a horrid nightmare that she couldn't wake up from anytime soon.

Luka's harsh voice came closer to her.

"It's not all about the sex, she's an innocent. In time, because she is willing, she has no idea what she is in for as she learns how I like to be pleased. But when I first saw Holly, I instantly knew I could love her. The problem — so did Kaine.

"That's when I decided I would have both the girl and crush Kaine — if I took my time. So far, so good. I've waited thirteen long years to take something from that bloody bastard that would destroy him as it did to me when he took over the band. *Hurrikaine's* my band, Rah."

"Yes, Luka." Sarah consoled softly.

Holly wondered about Sarah's instant sympathy considering he'd slapped her around the suite.

But Luka quickly reported. "I've enjoyed myself these past three days. I fell totally in love with her, Rah."

"I don't fuckin' believe you can Luka, she's another acquisition. It's not right to say you love her and then set her up so Kaine would think you're having it off with her those last days in London. How can you say you love her after the things you've told him? That you're sleeping with the cow, and how you thought he would have taught her to fuck better because she wasn't even any good at that. And that you would take care of that so he would get insanely jealous and hit you at the hotel, giving you a reason to quit and fly to L.A., with her. It has nothing to do with her Luka. You don't love her. You've done it all to teach Kaine a big fucking bloody lesson! That is not to fuck with the all mighty Luka Hunter. And you say you love her?"

Holly hung her head. There were the sounds again of fist against flesh.

"Owe."

There was a pause.

"Where's a cloth? Look what you've done, I'm fucking bleeding."

"Stay out of the loo, Holly's suite is on the other side. And if you know what's good for you ... you'll shut your fucking mouth."

Luka continued. "About the incident at the hotel. It was brilliant! I lied and told her that Kaine bloody gave her to me to take care of, Rah. Should have seen the disillusionment in her eyes when she thought Kaine gave her away to me. That became the turning point for her. She came running to me. And Sarah, none of what happened in London has anything to do with how I love her.

"Somehow, I'd fallen in love before that. Somewhere around the time at the castle, it happened. To leave her with Kaine, fuck, one of the hardest bloody things I've ever done. Next thing I knew, I had to get her away from that nutter. All's fair in love and war, and it was definitely war. I got her the job at CMT, was easy. Michael would jump off a mountain to please me."

"What made you think she would ever leave Kaine?"

"Because she never loved him. I saw the way she looked at me, everyone did. She didn't push me away or stop me, not one time. She's mine in every way. I'm the producer of her show and personal manager with a signed contract, her lover, and soon she will marry me as soon as I get rid of bloody Tessa."

"That will be impossible, Tessa's stubborn."

"After all these years, are you beginning to underestimate me? For instance, how about the European rags running the nude pictures of Holly and me. I'd hoped they would force Kaine into a deeper, hopefully, tragic depression. It cost me a lot of money to have that rag photographer take those pictures in Malibu. But they did the trick. Though, I'd expected the photos to kill him. Didn't you notice my hand?

Heart of the Hurrikaine — Mystery No More

"My headline. Kaine went straight down, and Holly came running into my arms for more comfort. Should have seen my outrage, especially when Tessa delivered the scandalous news. Bloody priceless."

"I should have realized you were behind that. And you're correct. Those photos, fucking devastating. Especially the one with your naked bum on top of her. It looked like you were boffing her. Thought I'd lose Kaine."

"Exactly as I hoped. But we didn't, the fucker's back and probably stronger since he's out of detox," Luka stated with disgust.

"He's not that strong. He has a weakness. His supposed love for the Princess Bitch. But if you convince him she hates him."

"I'm way ahead of you," Luka confirmed.

"I'm positive. Kaine's pathetic. When he went to the hotel to ask her to catch the plane that last morning for Paris, our timing was perfect, putting her in your arms and coaxing her to confess she loved you It took the last of his will to fight for her. By then the drugs and alcohol took over him. We need to do something as drastic now, but without the drugs. Luka, he was too close to dying."

"Seriously! That bad?"

"Worse. You have patiently waited for this to happen. But I love him, I always have. And Kaine loving that twat destroyed me."

"Kaine's never been in love with anyone, only Holly. As much as I hate to admit it, Holly is Kaine's Carrin."

"You fucking leave Carrin out of this." Luka snapped with a sharp edge in his tone.

"You realize what this means?" Sarah pointed out.

Holly looped the words through her head once again.

Kaine's never been in love with anyone, only Holly.

What was she listening to from the other side of the door?

Holly leaned against the door while the horrific revelations rendered her unable to move an inch. Luka successfully spun his diabolical plot to keep her and Kaine apart. He'd planned the southwest junket. It wasn't a spur of the moment trip. She wasn't paranoid!

Sarah continued to report. "My telling him about you kissing her at Friar Manor set him off, and I thought he would go after me, and then physically harm me. But like you said, being devastated separated him from the Princess Bitch."

"Stop calling her that! That's the woman I love and plan to marry. It's almost over, Rah. Our breaking them up gave me the headlines to charge double for *Hurrikaine* concert tickets because everyone would clamor to see if that concert would become his last performance. Then after I cash my check and our wedding, I'll have Holly. His woman, her love, become a father and Kaine can go back to England alone and fucking die for all I care."

Holly sank.

Oh no, he's told Sarah about my child.

"What's this? A child? You've gone and got the bitch pregnant?"

"No, you cunt, she's carrying Kaine's child. And the best part is, he doesn't know. Do you want him to find out? Are you ready to do what I say to keep them apart? If he finds out, he'll move the heavens and Earth to protect his child, his precious fucking heir. If he ever finds out, he's a father you will have lost him forever."

"No, Luka! I've taken his abuse for too many years because I love him. Lose him to her … I can't bear that. Okay, tell me the plan and what do you want me to do?" Sarah pleaded.

"That's better. First, I plan to propose marriage to her in front of him and the music industry, tomorrow night at midnight during the reception. When she says yes for everyone to hear that will bring the bastard down for the count. What else will? Then he can't stop me. He'll finally learn you don't fuck with Luka Hunter."

"You've done right well for yourself. But what am I supposed to do with the emotionally crippled Kaine? He'll be no good to anyone, especially since he's out of rehab. He'll dive into another self-destructive depression, and that will be it for *Hurrikaine*. He'll never make the American leg of the tour, and you can forget Australia and Japan."

"I can hope," Luka admitted flatly.

"My plan exactly!" And Luka laughed wildly.

Holly held her stomach and metered her breath.

"I got my money out of that out-of-time band while I could. Look at all the publicity I created with the Heart of the *Hurrikaine* to boost ticket sales."

Holly slid down the wall heading to the floor in the fetal position, sick to her stomach. The man she'd touched was ultimately a monstrosity of the worst kind. After all the warnings, Luka sucked her in easily.

He'd taken her, supposedly loving her, never understanding he was a sick and perverted lover and man. He'd repeatedly lied, saying he loved her, truly cared for her, yet he was more heinous than anyone ever imagined — or maybe not.

They'd all insisted he was not acting like the Luka they all knew. Apparently, he'd never changed his mask, the cover. Luka, the beautiful golden angel that fell from heaven, was truly pure evil.

Holly slid farther down the wall. Her head came to rest on her knees, burning tears streaming, her sobs swallowed to keep from breaking her cover. She forced herself to listen. However, she needed the rest of the story to know how to fight.

"I didn't count on falling in this deep. Love is something I never expected to have again. The instant attraction was there, she looked like Carrin, even sweet and naive like Carrin. I believed in second chances, but this time, I would protect her. I will not give her up to a fucking jealous and crazy chap, especially if he is Kaine. How mad, history was repeating itself. I can't bloody think about that. I have to stay focused, get rid of Kaine, marry Holly and get on with our lives."

"Yeah, and taking Kaine down makes it much sweeter, knowing you've got his baby too. Luka, how can you take his child?"

"Easy ... I have to admit my plan has worked perfectly, seemingly better. It took a bit of restraint on my part that first day in England. I had her wanting to fuck me badly. All I needed to do was point her in the direction of Kaine. And well, he'd enjoy fucking her. She has those lean, curvy lines and big bits. In the old days, he would have fucked her at the video shoot. That's when I knew something was up with him. He'd changed, couldn't believe my bloody luck. Did you know the bastard asked her to go on tour and marry him in Paris?"

Holly's heart sank, filled with humiliation. Her intuition was spot on all along about him. Luka primed her, auditioned her for the Luka Hunter Production. Nothing in London was ever real. Then there was a pause in the conversation, and Sarah spoke up apparently shocked.

"Fuck, no, I didn't. No wonder he took her rejection hard — especially, her leaving with you. Marry him. Fuck, the situation is getting worse by the minute. Get ready Luka. After all this rejection, he's keen on coming back for a fight. That means he'll take no prisoners. And I'm not confident you will win. But if you do marry her, I will need more money, Luka, because I will have a mess on my hands. He'll be on suicide watch, and even I'm not paid enough to nurse him through that."

"WHEN Holly marries me. And why would I care if he wants to die?" Luka corrected.

"I'm not paid enough money." Sarah persisted.

"You'll have your precious Kaine. And, you have the bloody nerve. You don't need any more money." Luka's cold tone said he'd finished talking. No negotiating.

Holly wondered if the nausea and stirrings in her stomach would hold on for as long as she needed. Her tears blocked her sinuses and becoming impossible to breathe.

"Kaine, oh Kaine," slipped out in a tiny whisper while shaking her head no.

"I want another five hundred pounds a week deposited into my account," Sarah stated confidently because she carried a secret or something on Luka to force him to pay more.

Not a good place to be, Holly thought.

"Or, what Sarah? What will you do? It's cheaper to have you killed, and that's a phone call away. And you of all people should understand I have done that. What will you do?"

"I'll tell Kaine ... he'll come after you and you can't control what he'll do."

"What's a recovering drug addict and alcoholic with a history of violent acts going to do to me? No court in the world would believe him if I ever allowed it to get that far."

Sarah scoffed, quickly to point out again. "For starters, I'll tell him all about Holly and this deception. You'd lose the game. You'd lose it all."

"You've learned well from me. But what proof do you have? It's your pathetic, lying word against mine. Me, the man that took *Hurrikaine* to the top."

"Not ... really." Sarah dared to say.

"What do you mean 'not really'?"

"I have proof of all your dodgy dealing like payoffs, the drug money, and about the murders. I have the computer floppy discs hidden if anything happens to me. Yes, you taught me too well, Luka."

Luka didn't seem to be ruffled by this news.

"Yes, I did? Am I supposed to be scared? How I do business is none of your fucking concern, besides the fact that you can't prove your stupid accusations. No one will ever find me attached to any of that. You're lying, there's no paper trail and no loose ends. And these days I'm more forgiving because Holly's love has changed me."

"Not for the better. Look at the list of despicable things you've done, a real change Luka. For the worse, if you ask me."

"I'm not asking you. I'm telling you that woman has sparked something in me I'd long forgotten. I haven't encountered these kinds of feelings in a long time, giving me a weak edge, a vulnerability I haven't experienced in over a decade. I can't bear to lose her love or her honesty. Even with Kaine's imminent arrival, she's been honest about her feelings for him and me. And I love her more if possible because she truly trusts me."

"She's a bloody fool trusting the devil."

"True, fortunately for me that's not how she sees me. I've convinced her Kaine's the threat. Funny, for once, that poor sod never had anything to do with any of this. He's finally cleaned up his act and fallen in love with her. Well, that love may cost him his life."

"She will find out one day, it's you, and how you orchestrated this whole show...."

Luka cut her off ... "She'll never find out about me!" He roared fiercely banging his fist on something solid.

Holly shook her head. She didn't want to listen anymore. She held onto her stomach hoping she would not empty it and give herself away.

Then Luka's voice moves to another location farther away in the suite. He raised his voice again.

"This is rubbish. Shut the fuck up you cow. I'm through reasoning with you. If you tell Kaine anything, I'll ensure you'll be without your precious Kaine forever. And you've seen what I do with loose ends — and I mean you." Again, the unmistakable sound of something hitting flesh again.

And Holly remembered Sarah down in the dark corridor

at Friar Manor beating on her as she listened to Luka pounding on her.

Holly fought the urges to vomit.

Should she make herself known and stop the vicious attack? Or, should she let Sarah get what she deserved?

Should she make Luka aware she'd overheard everything? But that would put herself and her baby in harm's way, not to mention the father.

Sarah's body continued to knock into furniture causing cries for mercy.

She begged Luka to stop.

"Please ... stop ... I won't tell...." Her pitiful words didn't stop the brutal attack.

Luka continued to strike her repeatedly.

"You tell him anything you pathetic cow, and that's the last thing you'll ever do. And I promise Kaine won't live to see the New Year."

"I won't tell ... don't hurt Kaine. He's been through too much, don't hurt him anymore..." she sobbed, between blows.

Then it was silent.

"This one is for Holly. You fucking kicked her, beat her beautiful face and stuck a gun in it. You'll be lucky if I leave you alive, you fucking tart."

Holly listened as Luka kicked Sarah again and again while Sarah's repeated her shrieks. And what frightened Holly was that Luka hadn't stopped and feared he wouldn't. That she would be the one witness to Sarah's merciless and violent death.

Then as quickly as Luka started, he stopped and ordered.

"Get the fuck out of here and let everyone, including your

precious Kaine, believes that he has lost his temper again and kicked the shit out-of-you. He won't remember with his blackouts. Not in all the years that you or I have beaten up his girlfriend's, neither he nor those stupid cunts ever caught on to us. They all kept the secret because they believed it would get worse for them if they didn't. And you're a pathetic cow Rah, keeping our secrets about that. He's never loved you, Rah. You have always been the hired help. To be thrown out with the rubbish.

"All your hope is dead. He'll never love you because he loves Holly. I'm confident he's going to his grave loving her."

Luka filled the room with a heinous noise. Holly couldn't decipher the sound. Then she grasped the situation, a laugh, a most sinister laugh as if he enjoyed himself.

He added, "Go, and don't cross me, Rah.

"I'm warning you once, or Kaine's a dead man…."

Chapter Three

MOMMA I'M
COMING HOME

L uka walking close to the bathroom door. Holly sat immobilized in a puddle of disbelief and horror. Every part of her body trembled, and her heart leaped into her throat. Luka could not find her here.

"If you think I'm not serious about Kaine," Luka said with a tone of intentional cruelty while he opened the latches on his briefcase. "I always have protection from drug-crazed rockers." Then he laughed.

Sarah's voice responded low and inaudible frustrating Holly.

"Oh, but I would use it. Remember, I have to carry it for security purposes. It would put a nice sized hole in Kaine, big enough to send him to an early grave."

Holly halted her breath. Her stomach filled with twisted emotions that forced burning bile to creep up her throat. She exhaled — *Luka was armed.* And as in London, the deadly threat came from within the *Hurrikaine* machine.

Luka's cool, threatening tone promised he would certainly use the gun. After everything, Holly learned she'd never underestimate Luka Hunter again. He would kill Kaine as naught if the opportunity showed itself.

Holly crawled off like a wounded animal, placing a hand over hand crossing the cold bathroom tiles into her suite. She leaned up against the wall next to the entryway, her head dizzy. Cold chills would not stop assaulting her body, racing up and down, skimming along the top of her skin. She stretched and pulled the lustrous fur from the bed and wrapped it around her for warmth and let loose with her sobs flowing uncontrollably.

"What should I do?" She whispered into Kaine's gift while Luka's words haunted her. *A hole big enough to send him to an early grave.* The next breath was short, and she closed her eyes and pictured Luka, her beautiful angel-eyed lover. She wouldn't have believed it if she hadn't heard his diabolical confession herself. That had been the problem — everyone else did. She shook her head, how could it be true?

Her thoughts were a mess and couldn't sort them to think clearly. She sat rocking manically measuring her breath, clutching on to the coat in the dim light of her suite. Hot tears burned down her cheeks and for a moment she wondered if the sobbing would ever cease. She needed to organize her thoughts quickly.

Luka set her and Kaine up at Friar Manor. Why didn't she listen to her intuition and stayed the hell away from him? Or believed any of Kaine's repeated warnings. He knew the black shadow side of Luka. But the one thing to come from his ugly confession was that Kaine truly loved her. London was not an act to him, part of a colossal money making scheme to bilk the world out of millions of dollars.

Her hand went to the place she needed to protect. She remembered the tiny confessions she'd made to Luka about Kaine and her stomach turned due to her shame. She'd been used by Luka with his filthy, twisted mind and the ways he'd made a fool of her. And Kaine understood all along that she didn't stand a chance. How many times did he tell her? Why hadn't she listened? What the hell had been the matter with her not to listen to Kaine?

And the photos — the dirty filthy Malibu photos splashed around the world. Never — did it cross her mind that Luka orchestrated them. His reactions that day at CMT perfectly timed. The joy he'd experienced allowing Tessa the coup that she put one over on the mighty Luka Hunter. No one did that. No one's mind operated that twisted, to be able to expose human beings to such shame, ridicule, and profess to love them. How could he have alleged to love her and then spread those degrading and humiliating pictures for the entire world to see?

He'd met her parents and betrayed all the trust they'd put in him to care for their daughter. And Kaine. The intended misery targeted him, and Luka rejoiced in his coup d'état. He counted on crushing him when he saw his lady naked and in the arms of the despicable Luka.

Her stomach turned and churned. Such a colossal fool she'd been. Moments of the ugly memories were interrupted by a gentle knock on the door separating her from Luka.

A strong bolt of fear shot hot adrenaline through her weary body.

"Luka," she whispered.

She couldn't face him. Not knowing the truth! Surely he would see she knew. How could she hide her contempt and bitter hatred from him? If he found out, she was convinced he'd kill her or worse if she didn't do, as he wanted.

Holly scooted up the wall and tried to take deep breaths, but it was as if her lungs collapsed, leaving her breath severely restricted and the tears wouldn't stop. She quickly dropped the coat on the carpet, kicked it, and then followed by kicking it under the bed. She rapidly moved into the bathroom and grabbed a hand towel, and then swiftly turned on the cold water to wet it while Luka's knocks at the adjoining bathroom barrier were becoming more insistent.

She walked sluggishly, wiping her face, pressing the washcloth over her tear-stained eyes. Every step jarred her nauseous stomach and any moment she'd give it up and empty the contents. She moved slower, like a condemned prisoner on death row. Her leaded legs stopped in front of all that separated her from Luka, she rested her hand on the knob. She closed her eyes, and she talked herself down off the ledge of horror.

I'm doing this for our future ... my babies, and Kaine's ... our future.

Holly grabbed a breath to calm her trembling and turned the knob

Luka helped push the door ajar.

He stood motionless.

The dim light from his suite backlit him. His tall, dark, imposing silhouette frightened her. He stepped closer and the fresh scent of him whirled in her nostrils. But when the scent of the season's peppermint hit her stomach, she quickly clasped her hand over her mouth to keep the contents down her throat.

He mustn't see.

Luka, stood tall, handsomely dressed in a black double-breasted Asset suit and a black silk shirt with a banded collar. How proper that he dressed as the executioner. And she saw him, the perfect angel — the angel of death. He'd shaved off his sexy three days beard. His silky golden hair clean, shiny and pulled back in a tail. Luka looked like a gorgeous angel. The most beautiful dark, evil angel ever sent from Hell.

"What? What is it, Babe?" His baby blue eyes filled with instant concern.

She stammered. "I, I'm … nauseous, and I can't keep down anything. It's been too much for the baby and me. Please make excuses for me tonight. I need to try to sleep this off then I'll be strong for Ian and Solange's ceremony tomorrow."

Holly hoped this excuse convinced him, as Luka pushed open the door, trapping Holly's limp body in his strong arms. His one-time loving arms embraced her, and another powerful wave of nausea assail her senses, especially when his sweet scented breath surrounded her.

"Luka," she muttered, twisting her face away from him.

"I'm sorry."

Holly shrunk from his embrace, predicting she would instantly empty her stomach as her knees started to buckle.

Luka held her up, gradually walking her into the bathroom. He placed the cold hand towel on her forehead and sat her down on the vanity stool.

"Holly, do you want me to ring the front desk to find you a surgeon?"

She looked into his beautiful concerned eyes. She saw the true eyes of her lover, who single-handed, masterminded the destruction of the one man that could stop him. Surprisingly, it was difficult to comprehend that this man standing before her, sensitive and concerned with her welfare, to be a confessed murderer.

Whom did he murder?

And his face glowed like an angel. She turned quickly and left all she held in her stomach in the commode. All the vileness of his time with Sarah came up over and over until nothing left. She moved and rinsed out her mouth. She shuddered when his cool hands touched her flesh. She struggled to catch her breath. She spoke quietly, unable to look at him. "Luka, please. I'll be all right, seriously. I've eaten something that hasn't agreed with me. I need to lie down for a while. Go, please. Make my apologies to Solange and her guests." She begged him but by the time she reached the end of the sentence, she didn't care what she needed to say. She had to get him away from her. She stood up as straight as her weak knees would allow, which promised to give out quickly if she didn't hurry and expel this loathsome creature from her suite.

"Okay, okay Babe. I'll tell them. I'll check back on you later."

Her stomach cramped again. No! He couldn't come back later! She couldn't bear to have him touch her flesh, ever. She would never be able to fool him again, and she needed time to decide what to do. She blurted out the first thing that popped into her mind.

"Please, Luka, I may be asleep. If I get worse, I promise I'll call down to the desk and ask for you. It's the exhaustion and a good night's sleep is all I need. Besides, you need to go to the bachelor party later. You can't disappoint Ian."

"I'll wrap things up early and come hold you."

"NO!" She spoke quickly. "…no, I won't get any sleep in your arms." She reached out and touched his evil face, stroking it as she used to when she couldn't believe her good fortune to find him. "Please, for the evening, let me rest, and know I'll miss you."

Luka didn't look convinced.

She hoped he wouldn't fight her either. She looked pale and ill, judging by the concern pasted on his felonious face.

"Seriously, Angel Eyes. I may be doing better soon, and I'll join you."

He once told her at the castle while watching the playback of the "Now That I've Found You" video that she was a great actress. Well, apparently she earned his praise with her latest performance that Hollywood would have appreciated.

Luka turned away holding her hand and concerned, informed her. "I'm not keen on leaving you like this, promise you'll ring me. I'm hesitant to mention this but have you considered this may be nerves because Kaine is due to arrive? Of course — you haven't heard. The nasty weather in London has delayed his plane. He won't arrive until tomorrow. Maybe you're more anxious to see him than you think. You're carrying his baby must make seeing him highly emotional."

The awkward tone hung in the air, and that drew the line where the beginning of his vulnerabilities started. For as confident as he sounded, Luka knew Kaine would win everything if he ever learned the whole truth. She looked into his cold blue eyes. Eyes that loved her in the most insane way. But his beautiful, shining blue eyes didn't look insane. More repulsion swooped over her again, and her hand quickly moved to her stomach forcing a quick confession. "Yes, you're probably right. This may be a case of *Hurrikaine* nerves. And, in that case, his delay will allow me to rest better. Go, enjoy yourself, say hello to Ian for me. I'll see you first thing in the morning." She hoped that he'd picked up on the point to leave her alone the entire night.

Holly accepted Luka's disappointment steeped in his eyes as he sucked on his lower lip, almost as if to pout. He moved closer to her. The sweet, sickly, scent of peppermint assaulted her senses. And when she saw his tongue quickly run across his bottom lip, and the pink tip of his tongue coming for hers, she held on, talking to herself, demanding she not faint.

Holly, keep your wits about you.

She chided herself quickly.

Kaine's life and the welfare of your unborn child depend on whether you can convince Luka you don't suspect him. In Luka's twisted mind, you're his intended fiancée.

Act like it!

That admission brought another flush of sickness too close to the surface, and she dropped his hand. She looked into his gorgeous eyes that wanted to stay with her.

Surprisingly, Luka backed off a bit. He'd accepted her deception. He did love her by honoring her request and needs before his.

He kissed her cheek, then top of her head and vowed.

"Until death do us part."

He closed the door.

Holly leaned on the partition, sliding onto the cold tiled floor. She'd been here many times. But this time — this time was different! She would preserve life. Protect her child and the father of her child.

A loud, striking bolt of lightning struck catching her off guard cutting through her shattered nerves, shaking her to the bone. The rumble of the thunder followed exhausting her reserve.

She pulled herself up, crossed the long distance to her bed and pulled Kaine's coat from under the bed, covered her head and collapsed.

She laid there crying, holding on to all she had left of Kaine.

What to do?

Kaine's coming — for her.

Tomorrow.

She hoped he wouldn't be too late.

Chapter Four

HOME SWEET HOME

Holly's head pounded with sharp searing jabs. She pressed her hands on both sides of her head using sheer will to stop the throbbing. The shock of her discovery not yet realized.

Her body ran hot and cold chills. She gulped headache medicine and laid in disbelief long past the sunset until the darkness crowded her. She smelled his breath on her, the scent of Luka, prompting her to take a shower. She needed to wash the evil and vile touch of Luka Hunter from her body.

She headed for the bathroom but kept going. A thought of reason managed to pierce through her state of shock. She cautiously entered Luka's room.

It didn't look like the room of a madman, a cold-blooded murderer.

She searched for the camcorder.

She found it!

Great!

Luck followed her because she'd unconsciously left the camera running. She had the bastard!

If he tried to fuck with her in any way, she owned proof. She may not know whom he murdered, but she'd have his confession on tape. Maybe, it would be enough proof if she needed to negotiate.

She quickly opened the package of blank video tapes sitting beside it, replaced the incriminating videotape with a new one, and changed the batteries. She turned it on and sat it back in a corner. She quickly left the confessed murderer's room, slinked into the bathroom and shut the door, locking it behind her. She took the videotape and hid it in the fur coat box. Luka certainly wouldn't have any interest in Kaine's gift to her. In fact, her deception would probably amuse him if he ever found out.

Holly turned the water on full blast, as hot as she could take, but didn't make her feel clean. She added cold water and washed all the places Luka usually brought her pleasure and then pain as the never-ending waves of revulsion swept over her. But there was nothing left to flush from her stomach.

She brushed her teeth furiously and recalled the times she touched Luka's body with her mouth during the unbridled passion. Her body went limp on her, and she slid down the wall of glass, loathing herself. She sat crying until the water ran cold. Her body reacted to the chilled water, shivering.

What should she do?

Holly looked around and turned off the water. She shivered ... too cold, never felt this cold, or ... alone. She looked at her image in the mirror as she exited the shower. Her eyes told the whole story. What a colossal, stupid fool she'd been. And behind that the terror that she'd have to surrender to Luka again and have his cold hands move over her body and take her in ways she couldn't form pictures. She hid her face in her hands.

What was she going to do?

Luka would come for her too.

While blow-drying her hair, she wondered how to face Kaine? She wouldn't be able to tell him what she'd learned until after Solange and Ian left for their honeymoon. She didn't want to spoil their magic moment, she'd have to hide her terror.

Could she be successful and do that?

She'd have to be.

More importantly, it wasn't safe to divulge these secrets when Kaine arrived on the crest of all the marital rituals. The other pressing questions? How to get through the next twenty-four hours without Luka finding out she'd found out about his deadly secrets? And as much as Luka professed to love her, could he be medically psychiatrically insane? He'd said he'd seen a psychotherapist. Or, was he a plain old cunning and clever murderer?

Any difference?

Yes, one was more deliberate and calculating.

She'd arrived, caught up to speed.

Luka was quite capable of having her murdered, simply to keep Kaine from having her. She needed to believe in his competence for murder. This wasn't the time to underestimate Luka again. She wished for someone to confide in, to check in, a reality check of sorts. But her information was too dangerous. This time, she was on her own and would need to act responsibly — too many lives depended on her.

Her long, brown hair hung smooth, shiny, and straight,

below the middle of her back. She needed to dress. But in what? All the clothes she brought Luka picked out for her. She ferreted out the single garment not given to her by Luka — the nightgown from Kaine. She slipped it over her freshly scrubbed flesh.

Holly called the front desk and successfully, faked a calm voice to hide her consistent fright. She left a message for Luka that she planned to retire early and see him first thing in the morning. She asked the clerk not to disturb her after they delivered a pot of herbal tea and a platter of assorted crackers with hot clear broth — to settle her stomach.

A cold chill rippled through her, and she shivered, would she ever be warm again? She wrapped herself in Kaine's coat and sat on the couch smothered by the darkness, recalling the events Luka described to Sarah. She identified his finely tuned hand in each scenario. Even the times she found him smiling, it was a smug, pleased smile, especially after Kaine's confrontation at Friar Manor.

Now she understood why.

Sweet Kaine. Purposely drugged, egged on, and pushed to endure the agony of her betrayal. How awful. How painful if must have been for Kaine to believe he'd beaten her too, enough to go to the dark place. She'd always known he'd loved her, but her silly, stupid pride and Luka, kept her away, or she would have been on the plane to Paris. She wiped away tears of understanding, missing Kaine.

But, on the other hand, she needed to note the truth, Kaine never gave her to Luka — as if property — for any reason. What a lie. Why did she swallow everything Luka spoon-fed her about Kaine?

Emily's words tumbled back to her.

> *You're not listening. I understand now,*
> *Solange spoke the truth. Luka has already*
> *brainwashed you. We hoped you'd listen to*
> *me. You're not, and you're not to blame,*
> *Luka is a master. He has you believing*
> *everything he wants you to believe.*

Emily. Spot on about Luka.

Again, she recoiled at the ugly thoughts of how freely she gave Luka her body on Christmas Eve, and then again and again, in the desert. She understood his focus. He'd been caught off guard by Kaine's sending his sweet gestures of love to her, defying Luka's mandate — that she was his. He'd needed to act fast, to seal the deal. She recalled when Luka threatened anyone who would dare to step between them, and she'd thought him dramatic but protective.

He'd been deadly serious.

And she remembered.

> *What you don't understand is, you're*
> *mine. And when I say that it's not in the*
> *possessive sense. I mean that since I'm your*
> *personal manager, I'm involved in every*
> *facet of your professional career. I'm also*
> *The Heart of Hollywood's producer, your*
> *show, for which I have you under contract.*
> *I also have the final say about what reaches*
> *airtime. Personally, we've been*

romantically linked to the bloody awful Malibu photos as lovers, because the tabloids cover our every move together. To marry me solves the rest of the problems. Your child will be considered mine, no bloody problem there. Given our history, I expect you to accept my proposal straightaway ... the next time I bloody well ask you.

And if I say ... no...?
But you won't, will you?
And the sparkle in his eyes was gone, his eyebrows rose, and was replaced with a new message that said 'don't ever cross me.' And so, he'd made it clear, what her future held for her.
You're mine...
Over my dead body...
But you won't, will you...

The words wouldn't stop.

What the fuck was she going to do about Luka Hunter?

It was midnight when the polite knock arrived at the door. Her first thought was how she desperately needed tea to soothe her parched mouth, and the warm broth sounded nourishing to calm her queasy stomach.

But then she hesitated for a moment.

The terror jolting her body, dreading the possibility — it might be Luka. He would find her doing well and want to touch her — all night.

Her nausea returned stronger, forcing the acrid bile to inch up her throat.

What if it's Luka?

DAMN!

Should she open the door?

She cautiously approached acutely aware that two inches of wood separated her from unadulterated evil.

She answered in a whisper. "Yes?"

Another stronger knock.

She cleared her throat and trying not to sound as if she felt well.

"Can ... I ... help you?"

The words sounded muffled through the thick wood.

DAMN!!

She cracked open the door a quarter's inch.

There, standing in the black, backlit hallway, a tall, dark shadow of a man.

Her heart pounded in her chest threatening to break through any second.

He wore all black.

Fuck, Luka!

She lurched forward to stop him, but he moved too fast.

He stepped into her suite, blocking her from closing the door with his expensive Italian shoe.

Chapter Five

POWER OF LOVE

December 31, 1989

Kaine.

He'd returned — for her.

He stood in a long, dark suede-rain slicker, holding a single rose.

She blinked.

She stepped back a minute, stunned by how powerful her mind was to conjure him when she needed him most.

Tears instantly spilled, running down her cheeks.

This couldn't be another cruel punishment. Another dream to break what was left of her fragile state of mind.

"You're supposed to be on the plane." She uttered astonished.

"I'm not. I called from the plane with the phony weather story to bypass everyone. I wanted to see you alone, My Lady Love."

This voice was real, unmistakably real. The light British accent a soothing tonic to her frightened and brittle nerves. She was positive she was not asleep. At least, she didn't think so. The cologne she loved to inhale, washed around her as a warm, familiar cloak, enticing her, calling her to him.

No, this moment didn't seem like a dream.

This man standing in front of her seemed to be made of flesh and blood. But dreams had fooled her too many times.

He stood waiting.

The moment arrived — he came back to her.

Holly's unstable legs moved a step, barely able to carry her closer to him. He'd returned to her when she needed him the most. She stumbled, half out of her mind and fell toward him.

Kaine caught her mid-air as the full, wondrous scent of him enveloped her, wrapping around her senses. And tears streamed from the corners of her eyes as she looked at the dark head of hair and instantly remembered happier times. Her eyes stung as more tears rimmed her eyes to fall.

He stepped closer, holding her up, she hanging in his arms like a rag doll. His expression filled with concern and bewilderment.

And she looked up into his gentle, deep blue, loving eyes that screamed he loved her but that for the moment he was more afraid for her.

His face came close to hers, and his lips barely separated, lightly kissed hers bringing the sweet taste of forever love.

She lifted a trembling hand to touch his warm cheek and pressed her lips against his again.

Was he real?

Was this real? Or, a trick that her terrified mind chose to play on her to keep her from going crazy?

His warm lips pressed hers again.

She lightly kissed his again in return. She tasted the sweetness of his perfect kiss, savoring his familiar kiss, the kiss of her future, and she drank in the strength of him with greater urgency by the second.

Could this be real?

Kaine broke the magical reconciliation kiss and hugged her tightly whispering into her ear.

"I'm relieved that I've found you safe and unharmed. Everything is going to be all right. I'm here, My Lady Love."

"You're not real ... you're simply a divine dream sent to protect me from going out of my mind because I'm not safe."

She explained quickly, unable to stop herself, not wanting to know if he wasn't real.

"No, My Lady, you're not in danger. You're safe. I'm real. Hold me ... tighter ... feel me, and touch me. I'm real."

"You've come back for me?"

She spoke timidly, holding her fear a moment away from becoming a watershed of unleashed torment if this was the ultimate revenge.

"Yes ... my beautiful lady," he kissed her ear and spoke softly, reassuring her.

"Let me take you to my suite. There we can have privacy. No one knows I'm here."

She nodded her head yes.

He picked her up because she wouldn't let go of his neck and she wrapped herself around him tighter.

She buried her head in his thick, dark hair that smelled

rich, wonderful. She chanted to herself.

My Precious One came back for me.

Her hand went up his warm neck and fanned her fingers into his silky hair, and she whispered into his ear.

"You're real. My beloved is truly here?"

Kaine stopped and with a confused look stared into her eyes.

He was so close.

Again he closed his eyes, his lips firmly pressed against hers, stealing her breath away. He opened his eyes and gazed at her.

"I'm real, My Lady, you're safe. I'm here, and I won't let anything happen to you ever." Kaine promised, his tone even to soothe and calm her.

Solange, she wisely arranged Kaine's suite to be at the opposite end of the hallway.

With his hands filled with Holly, Kaine had trouble opening his door. At the same time, lightning flashed in from the skylight that ran the length of the ceiling, and the storm lashed the building, blowing out all the lights in the hallway.

Holly panicked, hugging his neck tighter, flashing back to Friar Manor, to the last time when she'd been trapped with him down in the dark corridor. The scent of him triggered a jagged bolt of fear to replace her fragile joy. She needed to remember that what happened there wasn't Kaine's fault. The corridor was a set up by a deranged sociopath and his ever faithful and vicious assistant. However, this was Kaine, and she hadn't been alone with him since that hellish night. But she quickly reminded herself, she held the truth, Kaine never brought her torment, Luka did.

Kaine carried her inside and kicked the door with his foot slamming it shut.

Alone — with Kaine.

The room looked as if swaddled in darkness. It calmed Holly, and she glanced at the soothing fire in the hearth, all the light they needed.

The lightning flashed boldly and then the roar of the thunder followed.

Holly looked at his elegant and lavish suite. In front of the open drapes stood a shiny black grand piano. He set her down on his soft, comfortable sofa, but she grabbed onto his hand and wouldn't let go. The lightning flashed again and startled her, forcing her to leap and grab a hold of his leg.

"My Lady, what's frightened you?"

She looked up at him. The terror becoming infectious and spreading across his impossibly handsome face. Never would she have imagined Kaine standing here like this again. She caught her breath and looked away, surveying the room.

Yes, she was safe.

She gradually let go of him but didn't move.

Kaine quickly took off the rain slicker and dropped it on the back of the sofa. He wore a midnight blue shirt, a black vest that seemed to match his wool trousers. He kicked off his black suede loafers, stood tall and magnificent in his black stocking feet, and then dropped to sit on the couch close beside her.

She studied his face and then reached out to touch him while saying, "I've dreamed of you many times. And I need proof ... this man is you."

His luscious hair hung much shorter, layered to his

shoulders. He wore the sideburns and a new day's growth of beard. He slid closer to her, and he took her in his arms and held her oh so close. He rubbed his cheek against hers.

"I ... am ... real," as he stroked her head calming her.

Holly held on tight. Kaine sat with her until she let him go, inch-by-inch until able to sit beside him, but she never left his embrace.

The terror subsided.

Luka couldn't get to her. She was safe, he couldn't touch her and do all the disgusting things he always did to her.

Kaine sat, asking no questions until he pulled away enough to look at her face. His expression said he was weighing his words, careful to speak. Obviously, she looked terrified, but not with him.

Then who?

One answer.

Kaine moved away cautious of her resistance.

"It's okay My Lady. I want to get something ... for you. I'll be right back. I'm going to the fireplace. I'll come right back."

She looked at him. She shouldn't let him go. If this dream ended, he'd simply vanished — and that was an intolerable thought surely sent to break her.

Kaine moved quickly to the area in front of the fireplace and bent to scoop something up from the floor.

Holly watched his silhouette cast from the fire's glow behind him as a backlight. He held something in his hand. She saw his face laced with immediate concern. And close to losing it again, afraid this dream man might vanish, and any minute Luka would come after her, overwhelmed with a strong bolt of fear, she shouted.

"Don't you dare touch me."

It was then she realized he held the last rose. Her anger peaking, she knocks the rose from his hand to the floor. And then she bolted up, and in a shrill voice started screaming at him.

"Who the fuck do you think you are? Think you can waltz back into my life unannounced after the hell I've been put through all these months, think a few roses and pretty poet's words will make everything all right, do you? You think everything's all right?"

The momentum of the moment drove her, compelling her, as she stood, then moved nearer to him, to circle him, screaming at him.

"I hate you, Kaine Walker. Do you hear me? I hate you?"

Seemingly calm, Kaine's facial expression didn't change. His eyes gave nothing away as he deliberately caught Holly as she circled him. His unaffected expression and behavior served to infuriate her more.

And following the clash of terror and shock that burst inside her, she followed the swiftness of her weakening mental state. She tried to pull away from him, afraid he was going to do to her the things Luka did to her. She fought him and then slapped him squarely on the cheek. The harshness of her condemnation stung her hand coupled with a flashing concern she broke it because due to the sharp pain and damned intensity. She grabbed her pulsating hand and looked up at him.

Kaine stood stationary, watching her, his eyes filled with concern trying to hold back his panic.

She hated him and swung again.

He didn't move. But he sucked in a fortifying breath, gallantly bracing to accept her blows of anger and pain.

"Aren't you going to fight me, you bastard?"

He didn't utter a sound.

"Isn't that what you do best? Yell and curse at defenseless women and leave them lying broken hearted in a dark corridor?" She fell apart beating on his chest with her fist and sobbed.

"You left me ... you son-of-a-bitch. You left me ... and you promised ... you'd never leave me."

Kaine tried to put his arms around her to comfort her, but she shrugged them off quickly.

"I hate you, Kaine Walker. I hate you." She wailed as her voice dwarfed her anger.

Holly leaned into him for a moment, sobbing, absorbing his heat, his body. He seemed real, flesh and blood, Kaine, here. Not a dream that came and went in the mist.

Kaine, here.

Touching her.

Holding her.

Loving her.

When she looked up at Kaine, she found him looking down into her eyes. His healthy face with dark sideburns, his closely cropped beard, so magnificent. Damn, he was beautiful, her romantic traveler lost in this century. He'd come to take her away, far away, back to the safety of the castle. She pulled back, her loving feelings for him bubbling to the surface.

Kaine's sensual look swept her face and his heart-shaped,

kissable lips parted. His breath caressed her cheeks. He spoke softly, as if she a skittish colt, in his familiar English accent while flashing his dimples.

"If you hate me so much, why are you wearing my gift? My coat?"

Lost in venting her anger she'd forgotten what she wore.

"Here, take your damn coat! I don't want it," she screamed.

Holly stepped back in front of the fire and took it off, throwing it on the floor, kicking it to land at his feet. She hoped to make a statement. Instead, surprise leaped onto her face when she looked up at him.

There the firelight reflected his dark blue, smoky eyes, and she found him smiling. His eyes shining bright and carried the look to prepare herself, he was ready to make love to her.

His reaction perplexed her. And she saw his arousal filled the crotch of his trousers.

"What? Why are you grinning? I hate you, Kaine Walker!"

Her anger fanned again into a raging blaze.

"Well, I hoped you hated me enough to take my nightgown off too...." And he raised his eyebrows and cocked his head a bit.

Holly looked down to find she'd dressed in the beautiful, white silk nightgown he'd left for her in London. She didn't have the robe on, and her full breasts spilled out. And she realized the fire behind her revealed her figure. And judging by Kaine's arousal, she wasn't positive about what would happen next.

She looked at him, trying to keep a straight face.

She returned to herself as the fear lessened by the second, the terror fading, and then the realization arrived.

He came back for her.

The forever love in her heart struggled to reach the forefront of her mind as she tried not to smile, but his look of hopeful anticipation got to her, calming her. She broke down, sighed, and smiled at him.

Kaine moved away from her, strolled over to the piano, and slid onto the piano bench. He looked straight at her and started to play the introduction to "My Lady."

The notes, soft and gentle as she'd remembered at Friar Manor. He commenced to sing, and her heart melted. She did love this man named Kaine, with the forever love. No more doubt, no more confusion, no more fight. She loved him, heart, and soul.

His voice filled Holly's heart and then the room. She gradually moved toward him. The fire's light continued to illuminate his loving face. She saw his gentle, sweet love for her simmering in his mysterious blue eyes.

When Kaine finished the song he wrote to tell the world that he loved her, Kaine sweetly inquired.

"That song is for the Heart of the *Hurrikaine*? Do you know where she is? He has never stopped loving her, not for one single second of one day. If you know where to find her, would you tell her — he's waiting for her?"

The sweetness of his confession called her to him as Kaine walked closer to her. His cologne intoxicating and he bent down retrieving the single rose from the carpet. He dropped to one knee and looked up at her, deep into her eyes.

"I've come back for you, My Lady. You have my heart,

always have. I almost didn't want to go on without you because it's been lonely and cold without you.

"But at the end of London, I believed the one thing I could do was to let you go, and then I wouldn't hurt you anymore. I'm sorry I left you at Friar Manor, please ... forgive me but I couldn't bear to cause you a moment's unhappiness ever again. You once told me you didn't want a man that wouldn't fight for you. Well, I'm ashamed to say, I didn't fight hard enough in London. Well, no more. I'm here, and I will fight him for you. Believe me. I've come back for you. I will stay with you if you can forgive me and love me again."

Kaine handed her the last blood red rose, placing it in the palm of her hand. She saw the sparkle on the white ribbon tied in a bow encircling the stem. When she examined the rose closer, she found a mammoth diamond ring attached. Afraid to trust her eyes, she glanced down to Kaine. He crouched on bended knee, his clothes draped him like an elegant model's, and then he looked up into her eyes.

"I told you in London, now and forever."

He raised his sleeve and brought into view, to show her he wore the ID bracelet she'd sent to him.

"You told me those same words on the back of this.

"*I'll always be, Your Lady.*'

"Don't ever leave me alone again ... ever, because I'm lost and incomplete without you."

Kaine took a deep breath.

"Will you stay with me? Be my wife ... forever and always?"

Holly leaned into him. Light-headedness washed over her as she fell into Kaine's devoted arms that surrounded her and she ardently pressed her lips against his. She kissed him again and again as if she'd stumbled onto a beautiful oasis in the middle of a hot, arid desert. She held onto the beautiful rose with one hand and her beautiful man with the other.

Kaine leaned back off balance to lie down on the carpet in front of the fireplace. He took Holly with him placing her on top of him and then gently rolled her onto the floor holding her in his arms.

She gushed with warm, flowing love.

Kaine wrapped his loving arms around her, holding her tight, bringing her closer to him, wearing his own vulnerability, as if he too was afraid that she was a puff of smoke and would disappear. His sweet, soft lips caressed her cheek and lips like smooth velvet, telling her she was safe, confessing his love and adoration.

"You must trust and believe me when I tell you, I love you. I've missed your beautiful face, eyes and lips every moment. Sometimes I believed we would never be like this again, touching and feeling each other instead of in my dreams.

"Here we are. I'm real; you're real, we're holding each other, remembering the beauty and wonder of London. Those days became precious memories of learning to love you, reveling in you beside me, enjoying being inside you. I felt alive and to have it all become ... well, I feel too wonderful to speak of such ugliness. My Lady, I've never wanted anything in my life as much as I wanted you here, safe in my arms, kissing you, loving you."

Holly continued to lay in his hypnotic trance, within the sacred circle of his love, rejoicing in his presence and protection. Her heart opened to him, and the pain in her chest from missing him overwhelmed her.

Holly gazed into his eyes as her fingertips lightly caressed his cheek. She traced over his soft lips and then up to drag them through his thick, luxurious hair as if lost in a mesmerizing spell as if rediscovering the true magnificent beauty of him.

Kaine's eyes equally transfixed on hers. Searching her soul for an answer. He pulled himself up with one arm and between soft breaths asked.

"Does this mean yes?"

Chapter Six

WONDERFUL

Holly's entire body tingled with loving feelings, and she reveled in her loving spirit for Kaine. How much she missed his enchanting soft touch, his wonderful smile, his passionate love. Mostly, how wonderful it felt to allow her love to flow freely — to this man — she loved wholeheartedly.

"This means forever, my Precious One," she confirmed.

"Forever," Kaine promised.

She saw the delight growing in his eyes.

She whispered, "Yes, My Love," and she pledged, "I'll never leave you alone again ... never."

Kaine dropped down and placed his tender lips on hers then lingered.

She had her man back, and she held on tight to him promising herself never to let him slip from her ever again. She missed his sweet lips, his seductive tongue with the promise of love with each stroke. She missed his sweet blue eyes also full of passion and possibilities. She treasured the moments laying there with Kaine resting his weight on her.

She caressed him, leisurely stroking all of his face. She remembered every inch as if a blind woman, touching his every curve and crevasse. She traced the shape of his nose, his square chin, and his perfectly shaped ears. She stroked his layered hair, and noticed a few graying hairs near the temples, and then she followed a lock over his ears then and on down to his collar. She ran her fingers through his thick hair again as it fell like a cascade between them.

Kaine was real, here, and hers. She adored him, traveling the map of his shoulders and then down his back. She wanted to touch every inch of him, to remember how exquisitely he felt. To remind herself that her memories of him as perfect were for no reason.

Because he was.

Her elegant and romantic Kaine came back for her, bearing the ring of forever on a single rose. And though her body and mind screamed exhaustion, she moved closer to him with her heart open vibrant and alive.

Kaine's heat surrounded her, and she found herself drowning in his sensual cologne. His eyes sparkled with seduction, telling her he missed her too and life became unbearable. She understood him, the words he whispered in her ear, shared his deepest fears and hopes as his hand ran the length of her.

He too was gradually remembering.

Holly kissed him long and sweet, lingering, her breath light and short. Kaine's persuasive tongue filled her mouth, slow dancing with hers, reminding her. Loving her with their special rhythm. His gentleness, his patience, no hurry or urgency, nowhere to be and no one knew he was there. He sent the heated shivers throughout her body, tenderly calling her to him.

He'd waited for her — he'd returned.

Kaine's kisses became shorter.

She opened her eyes.

His were closed and a fan of dark lashes lying against the crown of his cheeks.

"My Lady," Kaine whispered between kisses barely opening his eyes that glowed with renewed desire.

"I've missed your sweet, loving kiss. I've spent every lonely night lying in bed, remembering how you tasted, how you felt. I was lost and alone Holly. I'm sorry I force you to leave me."

Holly started to say something about his being forced. But Kaine stopped her.

"Please, I need to say this."

He opened his eyes wide, but he didn't look at her. His gaze was fixed on her cheek.

"What ... I did to you ... in London...," he paused as if to choose each rehearsed word. "It had nothing to do with you. You need to trust and believe that, and you're safe with me. It's a long, long story and I need to tell you as much as possible.

"Soon, but not tonight. This is our reunion, a night of celebration. And I don't want anything to spoil it. But I want you to keep your faith in us." His eyes swept over to hers, laced with a light guilt.

Her body jerked from his disclosure.

"Through all the sensational press and headlines about you and ... Luka, I never stopped loving you, My Lady. I knew you did what you needed to ... under the circumstances."

Kaine looked at her with love and understanding. His eyes revealed his hope he read her situation correctly. As if he hoped she would forgive him for causing her to suffer. Especially for leaving her.

Yes, he spoke the vile name aloud.

Luka.

She stammered, jarred by the thought of him.

"Luka." She struggled to say, but the word shattered into a million pieces in the air. Her contempt for him seeping deeper inside her. How to tell Kaine?

It had never been him to cause her pain. Instead, it was the master puppeteer, Luka. When to tell him without his alerting Luka? It certainly was too dangerous. She grew into her common sense as the terrifying emotions quieted. In that safe zone, she made the decision for all involved to keep up the pretense, for the present until the situation was safe.

Holly offered. "Things fell apart quickly after Friar Manor. He was there — always there to pick up the pieces."

The pieces that bastard made happen.

But she couldn't tell Kaine, he'd become enraged, and she'd witnessed the destructive force of his anger, manipulated or not.

After Ian and Solange's wedding, she would tell Kaine every detail then and show him the videotape as evidence.

She suppressed her nagging guilt, paused, searching for an acceptable excuse for her behavior.

"I went into a deep, dark depression too because I didn't want to be without you either. I was lost and alone too, and Luka was there. Eventually, he coaxed me out of the darkness.

Unfortunately, I'd lost my job, he offered me one, and then he became my producer for six shows of *Heart of Holly Would.* Mostly, I needed something to do to keep me from dying inside, Kaine." She decided to add to her confession.

Kaine leaned over and hugged her, his eyes reflected understanding, letting her see because he'd done the same. He'd gone out of his mind too without her. And it all had been pointless.

Holly looked into Kaine's sympathetic eyes.

"I know it doesn't make any sense. But by the time I knew you'd received the I.D. bracelet, but by then Luka had taken over my life. I was unprepared for what I believed was Luka's devotion. And at that point, I hadn't heard from you and believed you, and I would never have a future. With Luka … I'm not proud of what I did. He led me to believe he loved me to the point I assumed there might be a chance for a future, happiness."

"It's all right Holly. I've been through this before with Luka. I've experienced exactly how he operates. Believe me, you never stood a chance."

She smiled.

More than you'll ever know.

How could a decent, caring man like you, my Precious One presume Luka to be criminal and heinous? But then maybe he did. Hadn't he always warned her? If she'd listened, none of this would have happened. Her complicitous acts kept Luka in the cycle of destruction. Yes, she would stop underestimating Kaine too.

Her response, "You're right!"

"What changed your mind?"

Our baby.

She wanted to scream out.

Luka's confession to Sarah, she wanted to scream out.

"You...."

"Me?"

Kaine seemed taken aback and added.

"Holly, I don't blame you for anything you did with Luka. You, my love, were manipulated, convinced by the master of deceptions that I was gone, banished from the kingdom so-to-speak. You did what you needed to, sweetheart."

Kaine leaned in and kissed her, allowing his soft, heart-shaped, velvet lips to rest upon the skin of her neck.

And that's when it happened.

The kick of life.

Their child rejoicing, happy its father returned. The baby moved again reminding Holly she had a secret to disclose.

"Kaine, there's another reason Luka sequestered me from you. Something...."

Was this the time to tell him?

When would there be the right time?

He'd accomplished her requirements, come back to her not knowing he was a father with an heir but filled his brilliant love for her.

"I'm not certain how to tell you this."

"What?" He probed smoothly, squeezing her tightly to encourage her to open up more.

"I'm concerned how you will react when I tell you. But it will change our relationship forever."

"Do you mean because you'd been … uh … intimate with Luka?"

And the jab in her stomach almost forced a cry of disgust from her. She'd forgotten again that she made love — no, fucked Luka in a most uninhibited way. What had he said?

> *It's not all about the sex she's an innocent. In time, because she is willing, she has no idea what she is in for as she learns how I like to be pleased.*

Again, she shivered picturing Luka's characterization of her as an innocent causing a prick of deep shame. And as awful as those ideas were, yes, his skills and sexual knowledge changed her relationship with Luka. With those ugly memories locked in her mind where would she find a segue into the beautiful existence of their child?

Her time with Luka taught her many ways to pleasure a man. And Kaine would certainly notice, and innocent or not, she would need to be careful in how she utilized her newfound skills and knowledge. But, she'd learned much from Kaine. As a world traveler, he'd picked up a treasure trove of ideas, and she smiled remembering his 'around the world special.' Yes, her combined carnal knowledge would positively change their relationship. But this child created their final, unbreakable bond.

Their child.

"I'm ashamed," she admitted as she threw her forehead into his shoulder. She kept her head down as not to look at him, as he lay holding her, almost rocking her.

"Luka didn't come after me until the night your first gift of beautiful roses arrived. Before that, we'd had no communication. I believed you didn't want me, and Luka brought evidence, the newspapers from Europe of you, showing other women, too many women. I saw you moving on with your life.

"And Luka was there, acting innocent, or, at least, that is what I was supposed to think. Your roses and notes, Luka saw them, and they alerted him to your imminent return to me. And that meant he needed to step up any plan he'd made to ensure you didn't succeed."

"Seriously?"

She looked up at him with of a look of, yes, seriously!

Then he added. "That recently?"

His voice sounded encouraged as his words vibrate in his chest. His eyebrows rose pushing his forehead as if sorting this information to reconcile the truth. He moved, allowing his tall, languid frame to place her gently on the carpet. She captured Kaine's full attention.

Kaine explained. "I was told you two became lovers in London, the night after Friar Manor."

"That's what he wanted you to believe!"

"I was?" His look registered puzzled as he released her from him. "Tell me why you say that?"

Holly quickly ran the consequences in her mind afraid to fill in too much of the backstory and decided to say.

"Honestly, I was too ashamed to face you. I clung to Luka for comfort. And he acted *nobly.*" And she laid the sarcasm heavy on the word noble.

"Said he would keep his distance. Didn't want me running from you to him. His plan worked, he's clever. You were far away and then there the despicable photos at Malibu. After the horrible photos, he kept his distance from me for months, baiting me, luring me in, and oh, how I fell for it. Hook, line, and sinker. And I acted like such a colossal fool, but you were gone my Precious One."

Kaine started to speak, but she placed a finger over his lips to quiet him.

"I realize how awful the photos seemed. Especially, in Europe, because they don't use the black bar to cover ... I can't say it. Emily told me you became reclusive due to the scorn and ridicule. It happened ... humiliating. You're correct in your evaluation, my being in way over my head. But one wonderful thing happened."

Kaine arched his back and harshly criticized. "Yes, those months in Europe created a new hell for me, something to forget. Nothing wonderful happened for me." Kaine explained, the sharp edge of misery lacing his words.

"But there was," she argued.

"When I returned from London, I went into a deep depression and illness, for weeks. I figured the illness resulted as a reaction to the cocaine abuse and lack of sleep mixed with exhaustion. But it went on for too long. And then I accepted it as a result of the way Sarah brutally beat me in Friar Manor."

"What?? Sarah?? Beat you??" Kaine instantly flared, extremely enraged. He even moved away.

Taken aback, Holly realized his sharp response to the news came as a reaction to hearing it for the first time. She'd crazily thought he'd known all this time. But then, Sarah certainly wouldn't have confessed or, let him see her handiwork.

"You didn't ..."

She stopped, deciding not to finish, staying focused and, move on with her thoughts.

"No! Don't leave me. Please, while I have the courage. I have to tell you."

"Sarah?" Kaine repeated, and his eyes swept over her face as if looking for the scars Sarah left behind. But those scars resided in her heart, no longer on her face.

"Forget Sarah. For a while I was plain heartsick, missing you and for many reasons, I was terribly depressed. For a bit, I feared I'd end up back in the sanitarium.

"But as it turned out there was another reason, and that reason was wonderful and a reason that gave me a glimmer of hope. It became a bright spot in my future to live for, every day. The problem, Luka found out at the same time I did."

"What kind of riddle is this? Sarah ... reason sick ... Luka knows?

"What Holly?

"What is it I need to know?"

"You're scaring me." His eyes grew frantic.

Holly watched the possibilities of her words flash in his mind. She smiled. These precious words she held were not what her magnificent Kaine would fear. She laid back, practicing the words in her mind.

You're going to become a father.

Her smile grew with anticipation picturing the sweet smile of satisfaction that would erase all the fear lacing his eyes. How much he'd wanted this blessing in London. And didn't Kaine always get what he wanted? She was pleased to be able to speak the precious words.

"When I found out you're going to become ... a Father."

There, Holly dropped her bomb, she awaited the fallout.

Kaine didn't move. His dark blue eyes locked onto hers. No expression emanated from him.

The placid smile she wore weaken.

Kaine's clear dark eyes didn't blink, then, he blinked. His ravishing blue eyes like Luka's, but thankfully they weren't, blinked again. He continued to look at her, and then he dropped his gaze to her breasts. His hand gently rose, reached out, and timidly stroked her breasts. The hand that taught her the true meaning of love, light and gentle.

"Your breasts are fuller," he claimed matter-of-factly.

He scared her.

Kaine looked back up, his gaze seeping deep into her eyes while his hand cupped and probed and then his eyes swept back down her body. His hand freed her full breasts from the strained silk gown.

She saw something like admiration begin to glow in his eyes as he stared at her teeming globes.

He bent, coming closer to her body, his mouth moved even closer, barely brushing her nipple that rose and ached for his hot lips. His lips brushed her again, the rosy peak firm and hard beneath his light touch. He pressed his warm lips against the rosy flesh and kissed her. He kissed her zealously, parted his lips, and surrounded the large peak.

Her hands slipped into his silky hair.

Then he rested his cheek on her other breast naturally as he suckled her as his baby would. But she didn't feel like a mother, anything but that. The fire between her legs blazed and the sounds of pleasure rippling from her throat told Kaine she his woman first.

His.

He moved his head as if shaken from a dream. He let go of her breast, then quickly kissed the other and then looked up at her.

She saw in his eyes a calm ocean of contentment.

He glanced down, over her breasts his hand following his line of sight, leisurely, and seductively. His hand stopped below her navel. There he stroked the slight swelling, where her abdomen used to sink into her back. His hand circled the sacred area, and he moved his head to join his hand. His cheek rested on her stomach, and his hand circled the area over her womb again and again as if hypnotized.

Kaine arched his back. His hair fell down her side. Then he twisted his torso to look up at her, and his eyes searched for hers, keeping his hand over the sacred place as he slipped up to her. When he rested even with her line of sight, he moved in closer, closer until his warm breath touched her lips.

His words, a mere whisper.

"My child ... inside you? Mine..."

Chapter Seven

MY EYES ADORED YOU

K aine's tone was not of one to question the paternity, but awe.

She smiled lovingly at him. "Yes. Spring."

Kaine smiled peacefully, content with the new knowledge. His remarkably soft lips moved closer and indulgently kissed her mouth. When he raised his head, his dark hair fell in his face, and he barely kept the jubilant tears in his eyes. He quickly wiped them away to leave his eyes shining radiantly.

And then something she didn't understand filled them. Sorrow, a great sadness. He would always surprise her.

"You'd thought I'd left you forever. And you carried my child, growing inside you. That was why you were angry with me when I arrived. Why you screamed ... I'd left you."

And she wanted the sadness to vanish, for the anger had reappeared, the hate, the murderous look as Kaine realized.

"Luka, that bastard! He knows! He expected to father my child!"

And Kaine was bellowing, scaring her. She swallowed

quickly, hoping he wouldn't do something rash. The tears streamed from the corners of his eyes. She quickly lifted a finger to wipe them away as she offered to comfort him.

"That was why I was afraid. I needed to believe and trust that you loved me. Luka convinced me you'd never loved anyone."

"He was correct. I hadn't, until you."

"Kaine, I'm begging, can you ever forgive me?"

Kaine lay motionless, a lingering tear escaped from his right eye. The hate in his eyes leveled, he'd returned to pure anger, but his tense body begin to relax. His hand quickly slipped down to her abdomen once more, and he rested it there as if waiting for his child to reach out and touch its father. His breaths ran deep. His silence unnerved and scared her.

"Kaine?" She cried out, almost afraid to drop her hands on his hair, and weave her fingers between the long locks. She heard the words reverberating in her body as he spoke.

"You've done nothing to be forgiven for My Lady Love. You've protected our child, more precious than anything I have in the world, besides you. My child ... our child.

"I hope that one day you'll forgive me for not being there with you that day you discovered you carried our child. I'll have to thank Luka for taking such good care of you in my absence.""

His words appeared civil on the surface, but Kaine's tone of voice was steeped in murderous intent.

The words sent an alarm through Holly, and she exploded with renewed fear.

"No, Kaine! Please, let's not tell Luka anything."

"Why not?" He paused searching her eyes looking for

answers.

She saw it flash in his eyes.

"You ... thought ... I was Luka ... coming for you when I arrived. That's why you reacted frightened! You were scared and alone, left to deal with him? I can imagine what he's done to you that you're terrified of him. That bastard has gotten away with more than enough."

She certainly agreed. And though Kaine seemed different, he did have more experience with Luka's past and how he operated. She would need to give him more credit. Her underestimating people seemed to be something she'd been doing a lot of lately. But, this wasn't the time to exchange information, there was plenty of time for that.

And to calm and protect Kaine, she decided to tell him a tiny white lie.

"It's not Luka I'm concerned with, it's Solange and Ian. Let's do it for them. We'll keep tonight a secret. I wouldn't want to do anything to upset their ceremony tomorrow. Anything that happens between you and Luka would upset their nuptials. There is plenty of time to set the record straight, the next day.

"Promise me!

"And Kaine, tomorrow, remember the worldwide press. That is another reason we should pretend this night never happened. They will be watching our every facial expression and hoping for a confrontation between you and Luka. And Luka will love the publicity."

Kaine hadn't stopped shaking his head in disagreement since she'd started her argument challenged her with his silence.

"Pure rubbish!" He decidedly argued.

"I want to be with you. I've waited too long. I promised I'd never leave you. Let me keep my promise, please don't send me away."

Holly needed to find a way to convince him, and quick. He shouldn't have the details all at once. She simply would keep Kaine and her baby safe from Luka and Sarah. No matter what it took until the situation was safe. Then she'd explained the complete and unvarnished truth about Luka, Friar Manor, Sarah and her death threat, and exactly why she didn't catch the Super Star, Hurrikaine's tour jet.

"Oh, my Precious One," she whispered while stroking his face, his beautiful soft face with the handsome beard. "There's nothing more I want than to stay with you. But you of all people can appreciate how absurd the press will twist the story. You, and I are big news, maybe bigger news than the wedding. How can we steal their thunder? Ian's your best friend in the world and tomorrow has to be his day — *his* day. You and I have to keep a low profile. Kaine, I don't want to be apart any more than you do, but I need to stay near Luka, as everyone expects."

And what she didn't say as Luka expects so he won't be suspicious.

"Then we can start fresh on New Year's Day. We can make a statement to the press together and begin our new life together. Please, I'm begging you."

Kaine facial expression clearly showed his warred over the clash of doubt and reason. Clearly, he didn't like her argument or the arrangement.

"At the stroke of midnight," she offered.

"Midnight? All right, I'll give you until the stroke of midnight. Then we will announce our plans to be married, not a second longer."

Kaine's worried expression said he wasn't convinced, plus something flashed urgently in his eyes.

"I saw you face, your fear, thinking I was Luka coming for you. How can you entertain the idea of being with him any longer since he's done something to scare you?"

And as frightened of Luka, as she felt, she bravely explained to Kaine. "Because no one can suspect, especially Luka, whether I'm scared of him or not. I have to pretend, convince him, everything is as expected. Believe me. I don't want this any more than you do. But I'm safe, I'm not alone anymore, I have you. And if he steps out of line too far, I'll give you a signal. Please, trust me."

"I do trust you, My Lady. It's Luka I don't trust."

"I don't trust him either."

And the idea of pretending to be Luka's lady caused her stomach to retch. And she saw the same questions in Kaine's eyes.

Holly had answered before he asked. "I can discourage his advances. He's concerned I'm ill. I'll continue to play it up a bit."

"Can you handle that bastard? He's always gotten what he wanted. And sweetheart, in spite of everything, that's you."

She knew that.

Well, *now* she knew that. And as everyone warned, she was the one. But for the first time, Luka wouldn't get what he wanted. She would do whatever needed to keep Kaine, her baby, and her future as a family, safe. Even if it meant continuing as Luka's whore.

She winced and closed her eyes. Kaine could never find out — not ever.

Kaine allowed a deep, beaten sigh.

He'd given into her. She appreciated that he didn't want to, but he did. And now she was like him, doing things she never wanted him to find out about, ever.

Kaine looked at her and then suggested as if a compromise to her absurd request of him. "Then stay with me tonight. Be My Lady again. I promise to be gentle."

Holly leaned into him, delighted by his firm body and more by his hard as steel arousal. A body she'd loved and missed for too long.

"You do Kaine Walker, and you'll have Hell to pay."

His look of astonishment made her laugh, and she whispered, "I'm not fragile." She leaned back and rested her head in his hand on the floor.

Kaine moved to sit up straight.

Holly followed, and sat beside him, raised her hand to his chest and pushed the top button of his vest through its confining hole.

Kaine looked into her eyes as if wondering what to do.

She used her words. "Show me how you love me. You won't hurt me."

She hated knowing why that was true. Luka, what a passionate lover, and expressive teacher. She needed to be careful and not drag Luka's twisted sexual preferences into bed with Kaine.

She searched Kaine's eyes, then glanced down at his second button. The thoughts of Luka stopped her from looking back up at him. She moved to the third button, the fourth, and the fifth. Next, she worked on the buttons of his shirt.

She sensed Kaine watching her and casually glanced up to see his expression indicating his uncertainty of how much to show her.

Gaining a bit more courage she invited him. "Show me how much you love me, but mostly, how much you have missed me."

She slipped the vest off his shoulders and then dropped his shirt down to his elbows, took out his gold cuff links and then tugged at the cloth around his wrist, dropping his shirt with the vest to the floor. She leaned against him with her weight, pushing him flatly to the floor where she rose up over him with renewed passion for her dream man, the man she'd waited for all her life.

Wow, he was gorgeous.

Holly paused to look at him. And her gaze leisurely swept up and down his perfect physique. She wanted to reach out to touch him and kiss him everywhere starting with his moist, heart-shaped lips, move to his neck and then feather kiss him down to his strong, perfectly defined chest. How deliciously hot to her touch. What a joyous celebration to have him to love again. Her body heated quickly ready for him. She'd waited forever for him.

Her hands shook a bit from the anticipation as she moved to the top button of his trousers and slipped it out of its encasement. She pulled the zipper down easily.

He was sweet — he too trembled a bit.

Holly reached in while she kissed him, wrapped her hand around the top of him exploring how wonderfully strong, rigid and virile in her hand. She moved the palm of her hand over him in awe, remembering the hot, velvety skin, hard, so hard.

His impatiently rose quickly and kicked his feet, to free himself of his trousers and then socks. Kaine, the most powerful singer of his time, laid beside her, waiting for her, dressed in diamonds and gold. The gold identification bracelet and the diamond stud earring.

"You're beautiful, strong, and hard," she said loud enough for him to hear. He might even be more magnificent than she'd remembered. An exquisite replica of a glorious God. Her fingers gripped the part of him that loved her into motherhood.

Holly paused to look at his perfect shaped, breathtaking. She melted, succumbing to the urge to want to taste him, to enjoy the strength of him in her mouth, to kiss and suck him with long luxurious strokes.

She moved over him.

The white gown sent for their wedding night flowed in a long trail about the carpet as she pressed Kaine's back to the floor with the same motion. She slid down his chest, kissing him down his stomach, leaving a trail of moist kisses down to the top of his hard love. There, her hand milked him toward her mouth and squeezed a drop of what created their child from the tiny opening. And the tip of her tongue darted out and captured the dewy moisture, and then again to coil her tongue around the top of his sex.

Full groans of pleasure escaped Kaine's throat delighting her as she captured his sensitive spot and lavished her attention on him. Kaine's perfect body started to squirm under her display of passion. Soon she would show him her full excitement. His strong hands eased into her hair and wrapped her long locks around his hands as if a rope. She'd succeeded in twisting him up inside as she wanted. She remembered the musky scent of him, the dark area that surrounded the monument of his manhood. Her hand caressed his flesh about him, the smooth hip, the curve of him, and massage of the pouch that swelled beneath the wondrous beauty of his strongest love.

Kaine moaned with delight, under the stimulation of her skilled touch. She moved in closer, laid her top leg over his, and wrapped it around him to get as close as possible. She wanted to crawl inside his skin. And she opened her eyes to see him slipping in and out of her mouth, neither of them in a hurry, enjoying the intimacy. His hand cupped her cheek as if to feel the strength of him in her mouth. How sensual his touch, how forgiving and tender.

Kaine stiffened, and short spurts of his essence poured into her mouth. He pulled at her face, tearing her mouth off him.

"Not yet, My Lady. Come to me, my beautiful fiancée." He forced between quick pants.

Fiancée, she smiled and then obeyed sliding up his glistening body, the gown slipped to her waist. As she moved up, she drug her full, motherly breasts, ripe and sensitive, up over the ridges of his hips. Then up and over the sunken valley of his stomach and then up the stairs of his ribs. She placed her legs on either side of him, pushing herself up and then sat up straight on him.

His eyes flashed with lust and grew wide-eyed, filled with delight.

"You're amazing, beautiful, My Lady." Kaine testified with awe and a bit of gratefulness that she was his. One hand surrounded her breast intending to play.

"My Precious Love, please," she implored, "they are sensitive. Your gaze alone can make me release. I can't take your touch for any long length of time on my breasts, especially my nipples."

"How do they feel?"

"There is a pronounced added weight, and my nipples are readying themselves to nourish our child. I've never experienced such sensitivity from touch to my nipples. They even change in temperature, or with the types of fabrics I wear next to them. But most of all, to your warm touch, your fingers make me dizzy and wet."

She'd learned about the power of words and they seemingly inflaming him. But the pads of his fingertips paid her respect by gently brushing against her once while she deliberately dropped down to smother him with her full breasts.

"Tell me if I cause you any discomfort. Promise?" His voice is shaky, understandably nervous, and cautious as a brand new father. Kaine turned to his side, holding her as she drifted to his side. He pulled a pillow from the couch and placed it under her neck. His free hand then pulled the gown off her.

"I'm excited to watch the changes in your body. My child. Wow, you take my breath away. I've never seen a more beautiful woman in the world as you, My Lady. I'm fucking thankful you're mine."

Holly was grateful too and for once, the word 'mine'

represented belonging, not owned, and sounded wonderful.

He kissed her neck.

She pulled her fingers through his hair, pulling it back behind his ears, and there the diamond stud shined like his love. She pulled back her hair to expose her diamond stud.

He looked at her and smiled.

She smiled back and promised. "Not for one moment did I ever take it out." Then she stretched to kiss his cheek, his neck, the top of his shoulder, any place her lips would reach.

Kaine moved his head down to where he lingered between her breasts.

She held him there, on fire for him, his testing erection stabbing the side of her.

As predicted, Kaine's hot tongue traced the valley between her breasts. She wanted him to latch on, but she would quickly pass Oblivion without him if he did. She hated herself for knowing that.

He kissed the sides of the engorged globes, the swelling on the bottom and on top, but never her nipples, and that became worse. She wanted that sweet release that blissful moment when he suckled them his way.

Kaine looked up, flicking the white silk that draped on his trousers and pointed out.

"You're wearing the nightgown like I imagined you would on our honeymoon. I've been afraid too long believing I'd never see you again. These moments are like a wonderful dream. Here we are, together, and you're carrying our child. Holly, I'm nervous. I'm afraid I'm going to hurt you. I couldn't endure that a second time."

Holly locked on to his precious blue eyes and pulled him

on to her. "If you don't love me soon, I'm going to have to hurt you myself." She lovingly scolded then flashed him a full, inviting smile as she relaxed on her back and pulled a reluctant Kaine onto her body placing him in position. His strength lay firm between the top of her thighs though his expression said he wasn't convinced he should go any higher. She separated her thighs more to allow him to fit perfectly between them.

He moved higher, the tip of his strong passion inching up to the entrance of the valley of her sanctuary.

The seduction became excruciating.

Kaine dropped his head. His furry cheek lay next to hers, his moist breath blowing in her ear and the words he spoke she'd waited for a lifetime.

"I love you, Mrs. Walker. No ceremony will ever make me closer to you than this moment. Remember, now and forever."

Kaine entered her.

She pulled him deep, deeper, then as far as she could. She wanted him quick, and deep, to fill her.

But Kaine proceeded with caution, inched in, aware as if to allow time to withdraw at any moment if he caused her a flinch of pain.

"You aren't causing any discomfort. On the contrary, you're good, better than good, wonderful, umm, better than wonderful, perfect."

Kaine moved quicker.

But not quick enough. Holly wrapped her legs around his body and coached him.

"Roll over, Mr. Big Time."

His expression puzzled, for a second. "My Lady, this

position is wise?"

"If I'm going to be ravished by you, it is wise." She braved and then smiled a wider grin.

His eyes filled with delight at the possibilities of her remark.

She leaned in dropping a hardened nipple into his lips, asking for a deeper entrance.

He looked up at her.

She smiled as if offering candy.

He opened his mouth.

She pushed her hips down onto him at the same time.

He felt perfect. To have Kaine in her with their child.

Finally — a family.

His lips sought her mouth, wet and pink from kissing her. She let go and moved harder and harder, faster and faster.

Kaine followed her.

She stopped kissing him and between frustrated pants, used her words.

"You won't hurt me. It doesn't hurt to love me. Taste me. Feel me. Show me how deep you can go. Love me, Kaine. It's been too long. I've needed your strong love for a long, long time."

Kaine responded, giving her all his love. He dropped his shield of protection and became a passionate man. A man exclusively in love with his woman. He acted like a hungry and starved man, seeking sanctuary deep inside her.

And she loved him, oh how she loved her man named Kaine. She moved him deeper, crying out as if in a stupor, locked in frenzy an octave above his moans of delight.

His arms surrounded her back, and he rolled her to the

side, no longer apprehensive. Then he rolled on top of her and lifted his head. The dark hair framed his gorgeous face.

And she watched him, watch her, as he entered with long hard thrust. She let him see the elation, the mounting rapture that he brought to her.

And after a few measured thrust, he seemed convinced his actions created excitement, not harm. And with a new determination that ecstasy awaited him within her, and not distress her, he released his passion showing her the way, happy to love her. He wrapped his arms around her lower back, and with a new freedom, plunged deep to reach the top of her. His incredible power and strength pumped her, harder and harder as if he'd never get enough of her. Higher and deeper he moved, until she lay breathless, her pants coming quickly to match his. She rode the waves of affection, lost in abandon and happiness, but mostly the heat of pure love. The waves shot from her toes to the tip of her head in a blink.

Kaine's lips feverishly attached to her mouth and their hands moving to anchor them as the peak of their frenzy shattered into a million pieces. She cracked open her eyes to find him watching her. She let him see the ecstasy he brought to her, the pure joy of having him back inside her and allowed a deep breath. Her magnificent lover, strong, impassioned, and thoughtful, filling her with his one-of-a-kind love. The warm seed that made them a family flowed freely between them. And they floated about in their bliss, kissing and touching and being one mind, one body, and then one love.

She knew they were real.

This man no dream.

They were in love. Open heart to open heart sharing their

sacred sanctuary. No longer needing screams of approval, no prodding's for affirmations to say it louder, no other man's name on her lips. She laid with her man, her one real love, the one whose name remained permanently engraved on her heart.

She whispered more words of love into Kaine's ear.

"I love you my Precious One ... and I promise I will never, ever leave you."

Chapter Eight

LOVE ME TENDER

Mysterious thoughts. Why was he always lost to them? Holly leaned over and pressed her body against his in the middle of the majestic bed in his luxurious bedroom. She treated her fingertips to a trip up and down his strong, sexy body.

She decided to ask. "Where do you go?"

Kaine smiled and pulled her oh so close and wrapped his arms around her. She positioned her head to lie on his chest and continued to caress his body.

"I'm thinking about our future. You, my loving lady, have had four months to dream about this, but I've had a few hours."

He leaned in a bit and kissed her meaningfully.

"I've never had a woman to dream with, what a wonder you are."

He kissed her again.

"I'm thinking about the next leg of the tour. It's in the states but doesn't kick off until early fall. Our child should be close to five months old, is that too young to travel? I promise you'll have the best of care, nannies, nurses, and we can have our own suites and the jet detailed to your needs. Chris has made it work, taking his family on tour, and now I understand why. I can't accept being away from you either ... my family."

Family.

Holly leaned in this time to kiss him, and blurry eyed admitted. "You will work it out, I can't imagine ever being away from you either."

"Okay, fiancée. Next, where do you want to be married? It can be as grand as the Princess's or as private as you like it. Money is no longer a problem, though it will take you time to adjust to the way I live. You'll learn about the money. I'm talking about vast sums that historically can divide, control, or destroy people. I'm hopeful we will use it to encourage and support. But we will live in a different way from what you've known.

"I grew up poor. My Mom always worried about the next paycheck because it was never enough. You must know the history of *Hurrikaine*, how we made money and then made an almost unlimited supply of it. That can knock you off guard because you never have to factor in money when making decisions."

She had a working knowledge of what he spoke about, from Brett and the wealthy clients at the law firm. And yes, living with Kaine was going to be a different lifestyle – and she was up for the challenge.

"I'll leave that to you."

"My Lady, we can be married anywhere in the world from Alaska to Zambia, and honeymoon anywhere else your heart desires."

"My Precious One, I've dreamed of many weddings."

"Well, you pick which one you want, and where to go, and it's yours."

"As soon as Ian and Solange are out of here, I promise I will give it all my attention."

"But not too long, My Lady, I want to be married sooner rather than later."

"As you wish, My Love."

"Next, where will we live?"

"I would never have entertained the idea that you'd live anywhere but at the castle."

"You know?" He said, sheepishly.

"That's the first time you've acknowledged that Briarwood Estate is yours, or that the castle is your home."

"How long have you known?"

"Since London, when Emily came to speak to me as your advocate, she gave me a tiny bit of Dunnehill history, that Briarwood Castle was your home. Later, doing research on the band for yours and Ian's interview, I read about the estate in the *Hurrikaine* history."

"I'm ashamed I didn't share that snippet with you during the video shoot. But I didn't want to overwhelm or confuse you. Briarwood is a big part of my life and as a lady of the estate there will be responsibilities and obligations, and I didn't want to frighten you away."

"I do love a challenge, and Lady of Briarwood Estate sounds wonderful. But what about becoming the Duchess of Dunnehill, and the peerage, when would that begin and what does it mean?"

"When? When the palace decides. The title will come to you, of course, as a result of our marriage and will be passed on to my legitimate children – and before you ask. No, I don't have any children that I'm aware of — this far. The first-born son, historically, inherits the land. That's why Briarwood Estate was left to me and not to Emily. And Emily made it clear that she doesn't care. But general decisions about the estate, out of respect, I consult with her.

"She's wealthy in her own right with her art pieces and *Lady Em Studios* around the world. You and she shouldn't have any problems with the division of duty or inheritance. And our solicitors will update the estate planning and business holdings. You'll never need to worry another day in your life, you and our children will be taken care of always.

"Course, there's Nicky, he's made his home there. And *Hurrikaine* has been profitable for him. Nicky and I are business partners in a couple of ventures under a corporation we've set up called LandFall Management Company. We call it LMC. He has other investment too. We recently acquired another large holding. To date, all we seem to do is generate money."

Yes, she knew about the all-important acquisition, forty-nine percent of CMT.

"Lastly, my sister, she has her own birthright and title, Lady Emily Dunnehill-Jamison. My Lady, in your case, has been an endearment from me. Lady, in her case, denotes peerage rank, as it will with you. Protocol dictates that you will be addressed as 'Her Grace' or 'Your Grace,' Your position in peerage is a duchess.

"It has been described to me as a position of a

noblewoman of high rank, which we will learn about in time. As protocol dictates, like you, I'm referred to as "His Grace" or "Your Grace," and together we will become, "Their Royal Highnesses the Duke and Duchess of Dunnehill."

"I don't pretend to understand much of it, and I stopped fighting it a long time ago. You will run up against it with the old traditionalists around the estate. Naturally, I inherited the title at eighteen, from Edward, my father, after his death. I tried to avoid it, but couldn't. I don't know anything about how it's done, and in the past, I've had no interest. The papers from the palace confirming my peerage arrived fourteen years ago, yet I've never been invited to any social events nor have I traveled in their circles.

"When peerage comes up, is usually rubbish, and in the papers. They love to quote the dissatisfaction generated from the palace because I became a wealthy musician, or as you've experienced it, for publicity.

"But the protocol? As the Duke and Duchess of Dunnehill, we will be guided, and you will be coached, as I was, about where and what to do if needed. It is amusing that two Americans will hold English titles." Kaine laughed and shook his head at the absurdity of that idea.

"As Lady of Briarwood, you will have a full staff. From spring through fall, we have a large staff to attend to the estate. It's not left to you and me. We are more the directors of the production. LandFall's business, I will continue to administrate from the castle. This will be a new adventure for us. I welcome you to become as involved in the family business as you wish. Or you can continue with HHW, or pursue your solicitor's license and set up a firm. There are charities. You can even look after the estate and affairs of a noblewoman. Whichever or whatever you fancy as long as we are together."

Holly suddenly remembered Luka's description of their perfect woman.

> *This woman, to become a wife, will need to manage the household and upbringing of the children, but understand that we are businessmen first, and can't be as hands-on as we'd both like, hopefully later, but not now.*
>
> *Kaine is a smart and astute businessman. We both have combined and separate business ventures — we run empires. We need a formally educated, professional woman to have a working knowledge to understand the commitments that come with running these empires. That special woman needs to be independent. She can't be clingy or insecure. Lastly, she has to be able to love us, accept the lifestyle and understand its harsh demands.*

Well, that was not a description of what Kaine offered her. He'd laid it all out, her future would be of her own choosing, and side-by-side with him, not waiting for him as Luka suggested. Again, Luka, so controlling, described his perfect woman, and now her good fortune never to be that woman.

She snuggled into Kaine and kissed his chest then said. "Forget the past, I want to focus on my future, our future and my new husband, and then our baby before I decided on extracurricular activities. And I'm at a loss about the peerage."

"Whatever you wish My Lady. If you don't want to deal with the peerage and obligation, I do understand. There will be a glut of media coverage initially around the wedding and then the birth. But we have choices. We can disappear. We don't have to live at the estate unless you want or I can commission a home to be built there, any kind you want. There is a lot of open acreage on the estate."

He chortled a bit. "It seems, when I picture leaving the estate, I'm a bit sentimental. Apparently, I've grown accustomed to my horses and dogs, the staff and even the enchantment of the dreary, gray mists and life of rain and seasons. It's different from the desert where I lived as a child or the West Coast where you were raised."

She lay quiet, dumbfounded by his portrayal of her new life. A gratifying life, filled with a greater purpose than she'd ever imagined, and nothing like Luka's subservient depiction.

"You want to build our family a home? That sounds wonderful."

"And My Love, if you find the English seasons too dramatic, we can buy, or have built, a proper home or homes, in numerous locations. Anywhere in the world you want, and we can go there when the weather in England is dreadful. In London, I promised to take care of you and I didn't do well. I'd like to make amends and honor that promise."

"My sweet, sweet love, don't you understand yet? Anywhere you are ... we are, our family is, and will be perfect."

"Well, you and I can live on love, but My Lady, our child needs a proper home, and our child will want for nothing."

"My Precious One, as much as I will always try to please you, our child cannot grow up expecting every wish fulfilled. We must give our child the desire to succeed, to create life, as you have, as I have, especially in the face of enormous privilege and wealth.

"I've seen what it can do, like with Brett, always trying to prove to his father he's better, or worse, worthy. Your child can never top what you have accomplished. Our children will need to feel secure in their life's path, will need to spin their own dreams and work for them to experience success in their own right."

"I'm pleased you speak as if there will be many children, and I welcome as many as we are blessed to raise. And you're right, of course, but please, no more of a mother's love and protection. You once told me to spin new dreams. I'm a man that never believed these kinds of dreams would come true, let me spin new dreams with you...."

"As you wish, Your Grace."

He smiled and cradled her in his arms. "Sounds better coming from you."

Holly moved in to press against his sweet lips grateful she'd found him again.

And he kissed her back tenderly and lovingly. He let her go signaling the end of the momentary bliss.

"Well, then, let me continue dreaming while I can. Next, the nursery. When we return to Briarwood Castle, you will need to choose where the nursery should be located, and then we'll have it decorated any way you want. And for the time being, we'll live in my apartment. It's large and comfortable, and will do until we decide where to raise our family."

"I see no reason to leave Briarwood Estate."

"Then I will build you a grand manor, befitting a Duchess, but it will be homey like the cottage."

"The cottage?"

"Briarwood Cottage, where Emily and Nicky live on the estate. It is a quintessential English Cottage, with all the charm but upgraded with every possible convenience. After you've seen it, you can decide for yourself. This will be an exciting part of my life. And I'm eager to share this with Emily. Wait, you don't know. She is pregnant too, and she will be pleased that we will be sharing family milestones with her and Nicky. Their child and ours will be months apart in age and will grow up together."

This wasn't the time to tell him that she and Emily already shared that secret. Or how Emily had all the pertinent details on her, or why she swore Emily to keep her pregnancy a secret from him.

He leaned in and kissed her long and lovingly again, seemingly unable to accept his good fortune to have her back in his arms again, much less planning their future.

When Kaine had exhausted the kiss, he leaned back and drifted again.

"Since our parents have passed away, we considered accommodating Nicky's family. They weren't fans of the weather coming from idyllic Southern California. They usually stay at the boathouse when they come for extended visits. Whether your parents come to live or for extended visits to the estate, we can build them a guest cottage to their taste, a house by any other standards."

She felt a few tears drop. He was considerate, much more

than she'd dreamed.

"You're thinking of everything, being thoughtful. Of course, my parents will want to be included in the wedding. I can't see me walking down the aisle to you on any other man's arm than Dad's. And yes, my mother, when the baby is born, will want to be there. And I do want her there as well. It will be difficult to keep the one set of grandparents our child will have, away. But beyond that, it will be up to them. But, my Precious One, I'm grateful that you have given them a choice."

"I welcome them, My Lady. Occasionally, Doug and Moonie, who helped raise me, come for long visits but have stayed in the castle. My Love, we will have a family and our home will be filled with love."

"I agree." Suddenly. "Oh...!" she yelped.

"What?"

"A kick … again!" She instantly guided his hand to the sacred area.

His hand laid warm, protective. And the signs of life moved again.

"Feel that?" She said excitedly.

"No, I wish I did," he said dejected.

"My sweet, sweet love, we have a bright new future."

He pulled her on him once again and hugged her long and tender.

Then Kaine whispered. "I was a dead man, until one night, a single light shone down on a beautiful vision sitting next to me backstage in the dark. And when you looked at me with tears in your eyes, I changed. And, for the first time, my heart opened. I'd been singing about you and waiting a long time for you to arrive. I wanted to take all your tears away, forever. I'd never felt so protective. You have brought me life. You're the missing part of me. I love you in million's of ways. I can never, ever thank you enough."

"Yes, you can, love me." She insisted.

"As you wish, Your Grace."

She smiled and allowed the tiniest laugh because he sought her mouth.

He dipped in sweetly. His spirit revitalizing.

She lingered in the strength of his love, pressing her, wanting her again.

Kaine broke the kiss and moved down her body dropping kisses every inch of the way, worshipping her body, down to the temple where the heir apparent dwelled. When he reached the sacred swelling, he placed a kiss on her skin and then laid his cheek there. He lay for a long while as if listening to his child spin dreams with him. And when the father in him gave up the conversation to the passionate lover in him, his hand moved to the place where it all started.

He moved his head and kissed the entrance to the womb, but not with the kiss of reverence, but with the flaming desire of a man with one purpose, to please his love.

And Kaine kissed her with the sweetness she'd grown accustomed to and then his mouth open and his warm tongue pressed her. As he moved his body to come into alignment with hers, he pressed her. At first, he pays homage to the mystery of her femininity. But the surge of creation moved him, his manliness wanting to pour out his love and then hunger for her.

Kaine took his time, loving, sucking, and kissing the way

he wanted to love her. To show her his extraordinary love, his forever love, and how he would bring her all the pleasure he'd kept for her, not using his skills, but his love.

His pure love didn't demand her vows to be screamed out in the dark. But to be whispered between the quiet sighs that begin with love's sweet kiss and then grows to a passion as such as he'd never known. He became lost in her, loving her, wanting her.

Holly accepted his love, opening wide and inviting his love to take her deeper into the fountain of his forever love. More and more of his heart he poured out on her. More and longer until her thoughts vanished left to sense and experience the completeness of him, wanting him, needing him.

She pulled on his hair, breaking the trance he seemed lost in, pulling him up, higher, up until he looked up into her eyes. And there, shining brilliantly, his forever love. A brilliant beacon of love as such, she'd never seen, a precious gift all for her. And her heart fluttered.

After he moved closer to her face, he spoke quietly.

"I'm afraid … how to love you, to make love to you with the child so close."

"We are lovers first, love me. Remind Storm or Savanna how much we already love him or her."

"You remember..."

"Of course, now love me. Show me again how much you've missed me."

"Storm is a nickname," he reminded.

"Whatever you want. And oh, I love you...."

The last thing he promised, "I love you two, maybe three, no a thousand times...."

Kaine Walker, rock star, shed his rock star image. He became a loving and caring man, the beasts in him tamed, his future clear. He filled with his new hopes and dreams but mostly love. And he took those thoughts with him, and he entered her. He pushed and pushed his way to the place he felt safe, complete and loved.

Holly held on to him and brought him as close as her body allowed. Her magnificent Kaine rose up in her. He brought the power and strength of him, and he released his strength, strong, again and again, reminding her of his invincible love filling her until she did the true words spill from her lips.

"I love you my Precious One, I'll always love you...."

She filled his face with her soft kisses and joined him in the place they created until she turned into shimmering gold, floating on the clouds.

They united, both guided by their mysterious love, gliding — one body, one heart, one love.

Chapter Nine

SUNSHINE OF YOUR LOVE

Holly relaxed.
Her body at peace.
Her true love Kaine ravished her and then joined her as one body, one mind, and one spirit. Their love flowed as if infinite while the lightning threatening to shatter the windows followed by the angry thunder that rolled over his suite shaking the foundation of the hotel.

Kaine's words, sweet, urgent, creating a new existence with his promises and plans to take her home to England, to live with him and raise their family at Briarwood Castle.

He confirming her prognosis that he'd be a wonderful husband and father. He'd finished checking off a long list to create a happily-ever-after future for his family, consulting her on all decisions involving making their dreams come true.

As usual, his plans moved quickly beyond hers. However, the one topic he didn't bring up — his plan on how to handle Luka. But judging by the venom that glowed in Kaine's eyes, it certainly wouldn't be good, but his confident attitude said after the confrontation she would walk away with him.

For the first time in a long time, her fear reservoir registered empty.

Luka couldn't stop them any longer.

She stretched her naked body long and snuggled in Kaine's hauntingly familiar scent that laced the sheets. When he'd turned to her with that look in his eyes, she smiled, overjoyed that he decided to relax and make more love, each more exquisite than the last, remembering her dynamic and passionate lover.

He loved her and satisfied his hunger with an exquisite love for her that oozed from his heart. When he lay resting his testimony was always the same, he starved for her.

Kaine held her for a long time, making the moments magical and they laughed, filling the room with exploding joy. And the smiles, full, happy smiles, overwhelmed that they found each other again, indulging in the sweetness of happiness and beginning their new life together, drifting to sleep spinning dreams of magical love.

Her hand swept his side of the bed.

No Kaine!

She opened her eyes.

No sign of Kaine.

She sat up with the swiftness of a frightened cat. Her every sense on alert.

Where was Kaine?

Holly leaped out of the king-sized bed. Had it been an ecstatic dream? Or, a long, torturous dream?

Noooooo because that would mean the perfect moments a

torturous joke and not real.

She quickly evaluated the situation, no.

She sat in a different bedroom, good.

She swiftly sprinted out to the sitting area in the suite and crossed over lunging at the piano. She sighed aloud, as she fondled the soft petals of the single rose, standing at attention in a crystal bud vase. She smiled with satisfaction. It bloomed, perfect in every way, like Kaine, reflecting his pure, exquisite love.

The white silk ribbon tied securely to the stem held the giant, pear-shaped diamond ring easily worth six zeros with the ribbon threaded through the finger hole.

She would need to speak to him about wearing a more suitable everyday ring, so she wouldn't have to have a bodyguard every time she went out wearing the mammoth diamond. But Kaine lived with a different expectation and his generosity toward her knew no boundaries. This was her engagement ring, signifying a new beginning with Kaine.

Her hand magnetically moved to settle protectively over the sanctuary where their child grew stronger every moment. She whispered to her young offspring.

"Your father's come to us. He's loving and forgiving, and he loves us deeply."

And she added

... *I swear nothing will ever separate us again.*

The weather took a well-needed break, no doubt resting up for its big finale. Holly looked out the window at the pre-dawn sky, realizing she needed to return quickly to her suite, especially before Luka checked up on her. If he hadn't already. That ugly thought sent a strong fear resonating through her, setting her nerves on edge.

Her intuition rose to high alert. And due to feelings of impending danger and foreboding from Luka's possible retaliation, she shivered.

How deeply she hated and loathed Luka with feelings once not thought possible. But mostly she feared his omnipotent power and casual knack for murder.

Holly quickly threw on Kaine's gifts. The wedding nightgown and pulled the faux fur coat tightly around her. She grabbed the single rose and put the sacred offering of Kaine's forever love, the diamond ring, in her pocket.

She needed to make it all the way down the corridor unnoticed.

She recalled Kaine told her he would be leaving before anyone got up to make his proper entrance. And he promised to keep their clandestine meeting extremely private though he'd grumbled about the wisdom of it.

Holly cautiously peeked down the corridor then ventured out.

She stood in front of her door with her hopes of keeping her secret, nervous, and shaking, realizing she didn't have her room card.

Holly smiled, remembering her impetuous Kaine literally sweeping her up off her feet and whisking her away in his strong arms. She almost needed to pinch herself. Kaine, her real beloved, returned for her, and she walked from one cloud to another.

She sprinted to the house phone by the elevator and called the front desk to send someone to open her suite door.

She slept until mid-morning and then phoned the hotel's

boutique ordering specific articles of clothing. She wanted nothing to do with the purchases made with Luka. She planned to shower and touch base with Solange and Emily.

She stood by the window analyzing the sky.

A black storm was brewing.

Chapter Ten

PRETENDING

By late morning, the clothing stylist left Holly with a basic wardrobe. Afterward, she wandered into the bathroom and listened near Luka's adjoining door. It was silent in his suite.

She decided to take advantage of the safety and turned on the shower. She stood in the warm, refreshing water, washing Kaine's scent of love away from her refreshed and ravished body.

She hummed a sweet rendition of *My Lady* to herself, delighting in her memories of the last few hours when from behind, came the cold hands of an intruder slip around her waist, so familiar, but dangerous. And when the hands turned her around, her worst nightmare stood in front of her.

She closed her eyes.

Luka.

He pushed his naked body against hers, his cock erect and hard. His cold lips came crashing down on hers, furiously and obsessively claiming her, possessing her, demanding she open her mouth. His stiff tongue pried opened her sealed lips, opening it cruelly, entering, and filling her until she lost her breath. His crude kiss suffocated her. He quickly drew her life from her like the emotional vampire he was. He continued to suck the life out of her, replacing it with his transfusion of darkness, dragging her closer to him.

She struggled, almost too weak to free herself, and Luka didn't seem to understand that she wanted him to release her. When he finished his deep, sinister kiss, Luka slid his arms around her, possessively closing in and hugged her tightly. Her stomach flipped flopped with revulsion, the hot bile rose quickly to lodge in her throat.

"Babe, I've missed you so much," he whispered as if to mean something special to her. His cold hands dropped to cup her derriere, pressing her hips against his stiff shaft that waited patiently to enter her.

"I'm sorry Babe that I didn't stop by last night. Can you forgive me? At Ian's bachelor party, the band jammed a bit. And guess what? You'll never bloody guess."

Holly nodded, acknowledging his obvious joy in his narcissistic blue eyes. There his brand of twisted love sparkled for her, shining through, while his hands glided freely about her curves, soaping her body into a lather like many times. But he interrupted his train of thought.

"Hummmmmm, you feel soft, Babe. Relax. Let me take care of you."

How much of his perverted attention could she take? His hands ... repulsed her. His vile fingers opened and prodded her private place. Was it possible that recently she believed he wanted to bring her indescribable pleasure and joy?

Luka shampooed her hair as many times before as if he

owned her. And when he'd finished, she was not surprised to learn how his normal expressions of love had been a cover for control and manipulation. She realized that this man was obsessed with her body. All the while, he talked to her. Something important happened to him.

"They asked me to sing. I suppose someone heard about Tucson. And you're right, Babe. I should bloody well return to the stage. There I was with my old band backing me without that fucker Kaine!"

She flinched at the mention of Kaine's name and the venom that punctuated it.

"I'm sorry Babe, I won't mention him again. Knowing you waited for me made it the perfect evening, except, of course, that you weren't there to see me. I'm going to write fresh material, and I'm going to record, Babe. And I have you to thank. You've changed my life. And I love you."

DAMN!!!! Amazing! Luka picks here to say the words.

I love you. No, don't — she heard herself screaming in her mind.

"You were right. I do belong on the stage. I've never loved anything as much as I loved performing … until you."

No, this can't happen. Not, not like this, she shouted in her mind.

Luka squeezed her tight as his hands moved once again to the place where Kaine entered. His fingers penetrated her, and he pressed his arducus body, his hands caressing her, stretching with a desire to fill the depths of her.

She hated him.

Before she moved from his firm, secure hold, he kissed her again. She detested his one-time sweet kisses seemingly unaware that he terrorized her. All that circled her mind ... she's finally become Luka's whore. Then, whore, she would be. She would pretend and make these moments with Kaine, picture his beautiful face, love his magnificent body.

Not this killers.

The decisive moment arrived as his hardness jutted her belly. Could she do this with him? And if she didn't, would he suspect something was up with her? Yes, he would certainly question her behavior. Convincing him that nothing had changed between them meant fooling him and was too important. But she would attempt to avoid his insatiable expectations and plead.

"Luka, I can't love you. I'm expected soon. Solange and Emily are waiting." She lied trying to placate him and escape.

"They've waited this long, they can wait a little longer." And his tongue harshly filled her mouth.

She almost gagged.

He moved — checkmate.

Damn! Used the wrong lie, she would submit.

Holly threw back her long hair. Luka Hunter wouldn't triumph over her this time. She was a player now, she would do this skillfully, and he would never suspect — until too late.

She struggled for a breath, and her body shook in revulsion as the tip of his cock ground into her with long seductive movements. He meant them to entice, but they made her stomach retch. It was too late. There was no escape. Luka would have his way, and she'd better be at her best.

Her knees went limp.

He caught her, holding her slumping body up and broke the kiss. He laughed in her ear.

"I'm glad to see I've still got the touch, Babe. Come here and let me love you."

Luka leaned her up against the steamy wall of the shower, like many times, but now, he forced his way into her, hurting her.

She wasn't ready.

She couldn't stop this assault.

She bit her lip and tasted the salty blood pouring in as Luka moved deeper. He lifted her leg at the knee, bent it and wrapped it around his waist, he wanted in deeper.

His cock, hard as steel, took a few seconds to make her body betray her. The moisture made it easier for Luka to move deeper inside her, closer to Kaine's child.

And the violation repulsed her. This act needed to stop, and she attempted to wiggle away.

All the while, he said.

"You're hot, wet, and tight, Babe. You feel fucking good. I missed you. You're the best thing that's ever happened to me. And if I haven't made it clear, I'm ... in love with you, Holly."

Oh no! He would expect her response, to confess the same preposterous feelings, to join in the safety of like confession ... to be part of his declarations of their undying love.

And she hated him.

Luka's dark-hearted admission fueled his fiery entrance. He jammed his sex in as high far as possible. His usual lust exploded as he moved in and out, hard, fast, she barely caught a breath. Luka dropped his forehead onto her shoulder, and he made his rough, demanding love with her while her facial expression was twisted in horror.

That said it all.

Kaine, where are you? Stop him. Please, stop Luka.

Tears ran down her cheeks against her orders. He would believe they were for him. And when he did see them, as expected, he loved her deeper. She expected this would be a moment for Luka to prove something, he would not love her quickly.

Oh no.

Holly's mind raced for a solution.

> *I must get through this. I can never tell Kaine that Luka has violated me. He would surely kill Luka. This has to remain my secret, forever so Luka will not suspect anything. I must protect our child, Kaine's and mine. They can come to no harm at the hand of Luka.*

Holly lifted her head back, threw her long wet hair down her back, wrapped her arms around his shoulders and pushed her hips into him. She allowed him to plunge deeper and deeper while she dropped her leg to wrap around his. She became Luka's whore, convincing him she was the one. And his words told her she wore her duplicity as well if not better than he did.

"You're mine, Babe. I love you. Oh, don't worry, Kaine won't ever fuck with you again, you're not alone, and you will always have me."

Luka's words meant to comfort, disgusted her. She pretended with her hips that his words of safety inflamed her as she swallowed the bitter bile threatening to spill from her throat.

He whispered in her ear, broken by his heavy breathing, Luka tried to excite her. "I have a surprise for you at the stroke of midnight, the second we ring in the New Year together."

She couldn't hear him. Her body was convulsing about his. And she knew she had to perform because Luka would take a while to find his ecstasy inside her. She was determined to deceive Luka. He would expect the spasm he needed to milk his vile seed into her.

He pushed into her, held on to her, pulling her from the shower, stumbling, pulling her to the floor on the thick mat that lined the floor outside of the shower. And he pushed harder and faster, squeezing each sensual cry from her lips.

She knew what he wanted to hear. He kissed her and moved leisurely inside her, giving her time to wash the rush of ecstasy from her, waiting to revive her and return to paradise.

Kaine, I love you.

She hoped her thoughts would protect her from Luka's outburst of renewed need.

But they didn't.

She hated him.

Luka took her in his arms, his lips pumped her mouth as his possessive cock moved, knowing when, and how much to thrust, knowing exactly what it took to bring her back wanting more.

And she hated knowing that.

His hands touched her everywhere. His kisses dropped onto her shoulders, his strong cock moved more quickly, which usually would have set a maddening rhythm to drive her crazy.

He spoke words of horror. "I will do it again."

"No! Please, Luka. Please?"

She made herself sick with her own act.

"Listen, Angel-Eyes, the ladies, are waiting. I've got to go." She insisted.

But Luka wouldn't hear of it.

"When I'm done."

His hand went up to the top of her legs.

"Maybe in a while, I'll let you go, Babe."

Words meant to seduce her, kept her prisoner and brought waves of repulsion, suggesting this assault might last longer than usual.

"Try to concentrate, enjoy, and let them wait." Luka's fingers gripped her derrière.

And Holly hoped to keep up her act, she needed to fake this and soon. His cock moved amazingly fast, and she did everything to stop the nightmarish images filling her mind. She forced a picture of Kaine's loving face and instantly relaxed.

"That's it, Babe, relax and move with me."

She brought Kaine's face closer, into focus in her mind's eye and it happened, she loved Kaine, his hands, his fingers and she moved with him. She wrapped her arms around him, and she searched for Kaine's sweet lips. And she kissed the image in her mind while Luka rammed deeper into her.

He moved her about twisting her body, giving her the benefit of his experience. Later he pulled her up and bent her over the counter, entering her behind never noticing her face wore anguish and pain. Luckily, he drew her back to the floor reentered again as she pretended a release.

But Luka would not let her go, he was determined.

And she hated him.

Kaine, sweet Kaine, walked with her in her mind, sat beside her and held her, loving her while Luka kissed her with his love flowing freely able to share all of himself with her. He never had a clue he'd been found out — it was too late.

He would not win.

She was not his future.

Kaine had returned to her. He was in her mind, here with them, no longer a ghost. Her body sensitive from loving Kaine, and now Luka, meant he would be able to bring her to a quick, final release and mercifully he'd joined her.

She was perfect, he said.

Luka's whore recited her line perfectly.

"I love you, Luka."

Chapter Eleven

CRAZY

Holly screamed out, "Luka!"
She tried to picture her sweet Kaine in her mind However, this man, Luka, held her, kissed her. She returned his kisses as if he was her heart's desire.

She let him kiss her meaningfully. This man, deeply lost in a bizarre and crazy love with her. And in spite of the pain given to him by Kaine and Carrin, he trusted her. He'd changed ... he'd said, naming her as the reason. But the transformation hadn't been fast enough. His horrific deeds, numbering too many made forgiveness impossible.

He kissed her with the expectation of a fiancé — his future. He proceeded unafraid, because she loved him, given her heart to him, trusting they would build a future, make babies, and grow old together.

She tightly squeezed her eyes shut. She couldn't bear to look at him. She turned to face the wall. But she couldn't escape his words.

"Babe, I love you more than anything in this world. I'll stand by you tonight. But I have to go to Ian's soon. The groomsmen are expected for the rest of the afternoon. I'm pretty well booked after that as I imagine you are too. I'll catch up before the ceremony. I'm expecting Kaine soon, but don't worry, I'll take care of him. He won't have a chance to see you. I promise you, he won't bother you ever again."

Ever again, echoed in the dark corridors of her mind. She forced herself to look at Luka Hunter Sinclare, the last fading memory of a golden haired lover that adored her. His long hair hung wet, he leaned into her warm body. She remembered the last of her sweet memories with him. She softly kissed his wet lips, finally, for the last time.

He never suspected her thoughts.

> *Goodbye, Luka.*
> *How could I once believe I could love you?*
> *Ever believed you were the one.*

And she let the last of the kiss drain away. He was a lousy son-of-a-bitch, and he'd woke up too late.

He was never the one.

There would be no more kisses of love, confessions of love and nights of love.

But to take care of Kaine?

Never bother her again ... ever.

What the hell did that mean?

She would need to stay as close to Luka as long as possible to discover his menacing plan. She looked deeper into his beautiful, sexy blue eyes, and she saw his devotion shining there. His hands went around her back pulling her to him. His touch made her skin crawl, and she screamed aloud, but it sounded like a groan of delight, but it was disgust. Her stomach twisted, and his gut-wrenching words squeezed her like a vice.

Luka released her a bit and then excitedly reminded her.

"I can't wait to tell you my surprise at midnight." His lips latched onto her ear, his tongue entered.

But she was on to this part of his vicious plan. To embarrass and crush Kaine, to pull the final power play.

Checkmate!

And she hated him.

Marry me, Holly, he would say in front of everyone, but especially Kaine.

And what did he say?

I expect you to accept my marriage proposal straightaway ... the next time I bloody well ask you."
"And if I say ... no...?"
"But you won't, will you?"

Luka expected that she would gratefully accept his proposal in front of hundreds of A-list guests. And Kaine? Poor bastard — Kaine — Luka would think, in truth hoping to destroy Kaine, prove that he lost because Luka won the contest, especially the prize. Because he always got what he wanted.

Her body lurched as his hands roamed her body freely believing to be bringing the fire, his pleasure. But his intent clear, to confirm — he owned her.

The question surfaced. Did she have enough strength to finish this unbearable ordeal?

Luka rinsed her and turned off the water.

"There, don't you feel better?"

Her answer would bring suspicion because the word better vanished replaced with words like defiled and violated.

How deep her hatred plunged.

Luka snatched up the thick fluffy towel to dry her and suddenly like the flip of a light switch, everything was different.

She watched him in the mirror.

She remembered how his lavish attention made her feel special. Now, he displayed his ownership, branding every inch of her body. She wanted this foul creature to vanish.

Luka stood close to her, oh, so close. And the beautiful face that she'd lusted on for months reflected in the mirror, mocking her. His face cracking before her horrified eyes, his grotesque soul rising to the surface like a killing virus, dangerous and deadly.

He frightened her, and she desperately wanted to escape from him.

Luka's once sweet, minted breath reduced to an unbearable stench that made Holly want to retch even more to turn in front of him, and empty her stomach.

His cold, cold fingers slid around to cover her abdomen where the heir dwelled, and he pulled her back against him, into the prison of his ugly love. He lingered, then turned her in his arms, and as the final punishment, he dropped his hand and slipped two fingers inside of her, drawing her so close to him.

"I love you, Babe, I do. I'd do anything for you. You've given me back my life. My desire to return to the stage. And most of all, love. The love I've needed for a long time but afraid I'd never find." And he pulled her closer.

Holly forced her arms up and around his shoulders. His fingers pressed inside her, stamping her, doing with her, as he wanted, letting her see she belonged to him anyway he wanted and to never forget.

He kissed her.

His tongue following the rhythm of his fingers. She couldn't take much more. Again, the bile in her stomach made its presence known at the top of her throat and with one swift jerk of her body, she twisted from his conquering grip, and emptied her stomach in the basin.

Luka held on to her, not allowing her to fall.

"Babe, Babe. You're not better!"

Holly looked up into the mirror to see the concerned lodged in his dark eyes. Her half-lidded eyes wanted to close and never see his grotesque face again.

He quickly placed a cool washcloth on her forehead.

Holly managed to say. "No. Please, I'm okay. A bit wore out from all your loving," she maintained and forced a smile. She continued on this theme, hoping to win a way out.

"Please, Luka. Help me to my bed. I need to lie down and rest a few minutes before I meet with Solange and Emily."

"They can bloody hell wait! I need to be convinced you're all right first," he said slipping his arm around her waist to take her weight on his hip.

Holly pretended to show exhaustion, as she stroked his devilish face, once the face of a beautiful angel. He'd been so handsome and those eyes, eyes that she would have done anything to please.

"Luka, don't let this tiny setback cause you any alarm. Go

on with your plans. I'll order herbal tea to settle my stomach and in no time, I'll be back on schedule."

Luka lifted her hand and kissed it meaningfully. Then he helped her put on a white terry cloth robe.

"Okay, but I bloody will check in on you. One more incident and it's the surgeon for you luv," he threatened as he helped her walk to her bed taking most of her weight on him. He turned down the bed covers for her.

All the while, he watched her with concern growing in his eyes. He pulled the crisp sheet up to her chin and tucked her in snuggly. His nurturing actions ran contrary to his true intentions, and that revelation distressed her.

Once Holly thought his concerned reaction was because he loved her. Now, she saw manipulation and ownership in his every move. She turned away from Luka to massage her curdling stomach.

Luka pressed his cool lips to her cheek.

"I love you, Babe. Never doubt that."

Luka closed the door behind him.

Chapter Twelve

WE ARE STRONG

S afe ... but for how long?

Holly exhaled in relief.

She lay quiet and allowed the tears to fall.

She'd done it.

Her confidence ran high that Luka didn't suspect a thing.

Kaine and her baby were safe for the present.

How long could she keep up this pretense? The answer arrived quickly, distressing and ugly — as long as needed.

Holly looked out the hotel window. The dark clouds seemed to go on forever with no relief in sight. The powerful offshore wind picked up, and it brutally pounded against her windows shaking the frames promising to shatter the glass. The twisted weather didn't care that she lay alone, broken and tormented, wondering where she would find the courage to face the rest of the day. How to face the impossible task to placate Luka and remain distant from Kaine?

With the ugly truth exposed, she felt ashamed that she ever believed in Luka. How truly beautiful he'd been in the early days and in these minutes, how quickly the sight of his face repulsed her. That observation made her wonder if what she truly saw when looking at him. And if the face in the mirror was what everyone else saw. She'd held on tightly to the invincible certainty that Luka was perfect.

They'd called it his spell. And, after all, her arguments about how wonderful he was, they'd conceded — that maybe he'd changed.

Luka called it her love for him that she wouldn't acknowledge — but everyone else did. He'd once confided in her that he wasn't as she saw him.

I'm not a nice man.

Another time Catherine pointed out that she'd always been in love with him, and glowed when she looked at him, 'a starved cat look' she'd called it. Ian had been confused too when he'd witnessed them together at CMT. He'd wanted the unvarnished truth. And when Holly offered the truth, that they weren't a couple, he didn't believe her either.

They all warned her to be cautious, to be careful of Luka Hunter because he always got what he wanted ... and how that was her. And she never realized he'd carefully locked her away in the tower behind the impenetrable shield of the charismatic Luka Hunter. She dropped her head, grateful and thankful her captivity would soon be finished.

"Kaine..." she repeated aloud. The sound of his name brought renewed peace to her, but it wouldn't last. When Kaine found out the truth, he would react with the strength of the omnipotent force of a hurricane for which he was aptly named. And hadn't Luka warned her as early as the video shoot at the castle?

Like his namesake the hurricane, he will destroy everything that is closest to him.

Closer than brothers, each told her. She recognized Luka was the closest to Kaine and his prophecy about to come true.

"It's you, Luka. It's you that he will destroy." She hazarded aloud, shaking her head because soon Luka would experience the true power of Kaine.

Holly trembled as she remembered Luka's hideous touch on her skin. She also recalled the gun in Luka's briefcase. She wondered if Kaine carried a gun. Would security insist? Did Luka or Kaine understand that to carry a concealed weapon in the state of California was against the law? Would either man care?

The revolting thoughts of Luka assaulting her wouldn't stop as if running on a loop in her mind. She pulled the sheet higher as she pictured how to punish Luka for his violations. Her personal revenge. How to bring him down on his knees for his heinous deeds.

Dangerous thoughts spun. In those moments, the impossible happened. She almost smiled as she imagined a bullet piercing Luka's chest in the place where a heart should be. His malicious life force would spill, his dark and evil blood that kept his black spirit alive. It would steadily drain into a puddle around him, and he would certainly die.

The picture of Luka dead brought her a moment's satisfaction.

Freedom.

Another bolt of lightning startled her, changing her

thoughts, and realized that she was fantasizing Luka's death at her hand. What happened to her? To revel in the death of a human being, no matter how low the life form? He needed her pity and compassion because he was a sick flesh and blood man.

Kaine, oh my dear sweet Kaine...

She opened her eyes listening to the ringing telephone. She wiped her tears and hesitantly answered. She sighed in relief — the familiar voice of Lucy. They caught up quickly.

"I have news," Lucy reported. "The daughter of the midwife that delivered both Edward Dunnehill and Luka Hunter Sinclare said to follow the birthmark."

"What birthmark?"

"That's all she's agreed to tell me. Wants more money."

"Give it to her and fax me the result. And hurry Lucy, you have a few hours — until midnight."

Holly made Lucy promised to do her best, hung up, and then joined Emily, Solange, Tessa, and Laura — Chris the bass player's wife, for the bridesmaid brunch. All the ladies expressed their concern for Holly's poor health that caused her to miss the rehearsal and dinner.

And that brought up the obvious topic when Solange stated.

"You will see Kaine soon. And I hope this news is not distressing. I hoped to relieve stress from one having to approach the other. Therefore, I've paired you with Kaine. As the best man, he will lead the wedding procession. How does that news make you feel?"

Holly didn't have the answer they looked for and keep everyone safe without giving them any reason to begin to act differently around Luka, tipping him off to a change in the program.

"I came with Luka, why am I not paired with him?"

"Because he's married to Tessa. She has the honor of walking with him," Solange said.

"Some fucking honor," Tessa complained. "I'd rather be thrown in a bag with a bloody viper!"

This was when Solange decides to reveal that Luka is married! If she'd said those important life-changing words last summer, backstage at Wembley Stadium, much pain could have been avoided. And tonight, Holly needed to keep up the pretense and ask.

"Solange, you have no one else to pair with Kaine or me?"

"Of course not. We've all agreed, including Ian that you needed contact with Kaine. Please don't hate us. We have your best interest at heart." Solange begged.

"Has Luka been told about this arrangement?" Holly asked guardedly because Luka, that bastard, conveniently left out that he was aware of her recent pairing with Kaine.

"Ian told him last night at the rehearsal and Luka seemed to take it in stride," Solange confirmed.

Holly looked to Tessa and asked. "He's accepted this arrangement? No different reaction from Luka last night?"

"No," Tessa answered and then added, "He didn't mention it during dinner, and afterward I retired early."

That was it. Because Luka heard of her pairing with Kaine, he played the sex and ownership card with her in the shower.

That bastard had tested her again.

I'm expecting Kaine soon, but don't worry, I'll take care of him so he doesn't have a chance to see you. I promise you, he won't bother you ever again.

Luka didn't trust her!

He'd planned to find out if she'd been in contact with anyone. He'd figured she would have corrected his admission. To tell him she would see Kaine due to their unexpected pairing.

That bastard!

He was beneath contempt.

She looked at Solange, the most beautiful bride-to-be.

"This is your day Solange, and I can't say that I'm comfortable walking with Kaine when I'm clearly here with Luka. But I don't want to cause any problems today. I will do what I can to honor your moment and be as gracious as I can be and walk down the aisle with Kaine."

Round one settled.

She would walk with Kaine. Apparently, Luka hadn't objected or forced a change in the procession arrangements. Therefore, she didn't have to skirt that problem with him anymore. But the bride and bridesmaids had warmed up because they all wanted to say something.

They reached the banquet table set for the bride and her attendants. Everyone took their place, and Holly hoped they'd move on to talk about what women did on these occasions — of love, family and, of course, the honeymoon.

But nuptial dreams were not what was on these ladies mind.

Emily went first. "My brother is due anytime. Holly, I do hope you have you changed your mind about him?"

Solange, quick to join in the collusion offered, "I can arrange a private meeting. I can give you all the time needed to reconnect with Kaine. He does love you with all his heart."

Tessa wasn't far behind in jumping on the bandwagon.

"This may sound contradictory to my usual banter, but I agree. You need to meet privately with Kaine straightaway or do whatever is necessary to reunite with him. I speak from experience. Luka will never love you like Kaine can."

It turned into a free-for-all with each woman making her case, talking over each other. But they meant the attack to be loving, and they each cared about her future.

Especially Emily. She flashed those blue so blue Kaine eyes that held her secret that Holly carried the heir apparent.

These loving women were imprisoned with secrets of Luka, and no way to divulge that their hopes and dreams for Kaine, a man they all loved dearly, would come true with Holly, and soon — they hoped.

Holly couldn't let it slip that their hero had indeed followed his heart. He'd returned to her. That together they'd made the strong connection that not even Luka could break. Kaine loved her and his child. His blood flowed through her body, the blood of the *Hurrikaine*, and that said it all.

She wanted to put the ladies at ease, but all she was free to offer would be anything but comforting.

"I'm here with Luka and expected to attend the reception with him."

Holly hated the disappointment that spread across their faces. And again the assault of how could she? Was she blind to how much Kaine loved her? And, of course, the favorite topic — the evil Luka.

She agreed with them on that topic.

They'd all be surprised to learn the depth of his evil. Or, maybe not. After all, from the beginning each lady warned her. Her blindness and naiveté had been the problem, her inability to accept Luka Hunter as manipulative and powerful as he was. She understood. She'd bet they all owned their Luka Hunter stories they never wanted to see the light of day. And that made her wonder what he held over each of these women.

Emily, Kaine's sister, what happened for her to be bitter and suspicious?

Solange, admitted to a brief affair, but how brief and what happened?

And, of course, Tessa, her bad luck to have her jaw broken by the supposed Blackout King, the ever destructive Kaine, and yet loved Kaine in spite of that. She would be surprised to learn that his attack on her was fabricated and manufactured by Sarah or Luka.

One of them broke her jaw. And Tess's other misfortune was to be married to Luka, and might mean losing her life's work, the Asset collection, to him. What ring of Hell had she been through with him?

Luka's far reaching hand of criminal activity now held her. Such a fool. She was bound by contracts because he owned her show, and she'd pledged to marry him. And she didn't want to consider the long list and kinds of leverage Luka held against Kaine, Ian, and Nicky.

Ian dropped all his prenuptial engagements because Luka

summoned him to L.A., to do HHW, and then sent him as an errand boy on to England. What did Luka have on him to force Ian to get on that plane?

Sarah never had a chance, always under Luka's thumb. As they all had — correction, as they all still were. Because everyone worried about Luka. What would he do when Kaine arrived? Not the other way.

And then she realized that they were all convinced that Luka was stronger that he would win this game prize. That he'd ensured that Holly would never be taken from him. They were all aware of his ability for destruction.

They all waited.

The showdown approaching.

Chapter Thirteen

MOMENTS IN LOVE

Everyone associated with the band *Hurrikaine* wondered what would happen when Kaine and Luka came face-to-face, knowing one would win. Most importantly, who would walk away and who'd be destroyed.

They'd all been incapable of beating Luka, and apparently, the unbelievable task rested on the shoulders of the one man that might. This table rooted for Kaine. But she'd met people that rooted for Luka. What the ladies didn't understand, Luka may have won the earlier rounds, but this was the last, and he would never win. Luka created the one thing that he was powerless to break or control — the *heart* of the *Hurrikaine.* He'd never break her heart that loved Kaine forever and always … until death do they part.

The luncheon failed to proceed in the particular direction that Holly hoped, wanting to keep the conversation off her and Kaine, and instead cast a black cloud over the women.

She wanted the day to be a time of celebration and joy. Instead, trepidation and apprehension ate away at these sweet, wonderful women. Each wondering which of the two dynamic and powerful men fighting would walk away with her. And how would the results of that battle affect them?

How had this happened?

After the luncheon, the women quietly trailed Solange to her suite to ready themselves for the big moment. On the way to the bathroom, Tessa cornered Holly and closed the door.

"After all our warnings? Holly, I didn't want to tell them, they are to upset. I can't believe it's true. You're aware Luka, and I spoke. He claims you're going to marry him first of the year. Tell me it's rubbish!"

"He's mentioned it, Tessa. He's not serious," she answered trying to keep a delicate balance between the truth and a lie.

But Tessa wouldn't listen. Her tone of voice became high and frantic. "Oh, he's serious, deadly serious. I never thought you were a nutter! You're too smart for this Holly. I've been clear with you — the bloody fuckers dangerous.

"In fact, off the record, he's threatened my life. I need someone to investigate if something happens to me one day. He said if I don't comply with his terms in the divorce and give him Asset, something will happen to me. I'd rather kill the bastard first."

Get in line, Holly thought as Tessa continued.

"I've put in sweat and blood to make Asset a success."

"I do understand Tessa," she reassured taking the trembling woman in her arms. Yes, Tessa feared her own reaction to Luka.

Holly proposed. "Maybe, Luka's all talk? Surely he wouldn't injure you?"

Empty words, she didn't dare admit were lies because

she'd overheard him threaten Tessa, and he wasn't joking.

"Holly. Holly!" Tessa blurted out, stepped back, and stroking her own long luscious black hair.

"You're naiveté astounds me. I won't say anymore. I don't wish to spoil Solange's day. But things are not right with Luka. Meet me tonight at midnight in your suite. We can talk after Solange and Ian have left. Until then, remember, this threat isn't over by a long shot. Luka's up to something, I can sense it. Watch out!"

Tessa turned on her heel and left Holly with her thoughts.

What an understatement! Watching out — exactly what Holly planned to do for everyone concerned.

A few moments later there came a knock at the door, at the same time, a bolt of lightning tore through the sky. The loud crackling sound made Holly jump. Her worn and frayed nerves concerned her. How much pressure should she allow before the stress affected her unborn child?

She entered the main room of Solange's suite, instantly relieved to find a legion of manicurists, hairstylists, and make-up artists. Their presence should keep the conversation off her and Kaine.

Holly settled in for the afternoon of pampering, looking forward to the soothing rituals. She needed to be indulged. But she needed to plan a workable scheme to flush Luka out of his suite and then get the evidence — the tape out of the video camcorder. Then she would replace it with a fresh one while she waited for the other shoe to drop.

Soon everyone would don the bridesmaid's gowns. But Holly needed to make a stop first. She quietly spoke to Emily about having to step away for a moment. She quickly darted into her suite and then she crossed to the bath and leaned against the adjoining door to Luka's.

Dead silence.

Pleased Luka's duties with the groomsmen kept him away, she quickly took the camcorder from the corner where she'd left it and made the necessary changes of batteries and tape. Returned it, took the used tape, and quickly placed it in the Asset box with the other. She listened at her door, the corridor quiet, except for the sounds of the rain pounding on the skylights.

Holly quickly rejoined the pampered bridesmaids in Solange's suite. She sat thinking.

At least, if anything happens, I'll have the bastard on videotape.

She sat back hoping she'd checked off each concern on her long list and decided to relax.

By late afternoon, the bridesmaids finally gave up trying to reason with her and their spirits picked up ready to celebrate by the time they dropped their Asset gowns over their heads.

Standing behind Emily, Holly took the opportunity to venture a question.

"Do you have any birthmarks?"

Emily turned with the most inquisitive look scrunching her eyebrows. "That's a curious thing to ask."

"Sounds odd." She deflected. "I see this little mark on your upper shoulder, and it made me wonder if Kaine had one?"

"It's odd you ask. This mark is on both of our shoulders. It is the family mark of Dunnehill, Father used to say."

Holly tried to remember Kaine's shoulders.

"Kaine's?" Holly queried as if asking where it was placed.

Emily looked troubled.

"It's located where Father beat him. There is a tiny part visible to the eye. The marks surprised both of us that each of us bore the mark. We've never told anyone."

DAMN!

Follow the birthmark.

It started to make sense. Holly remembered and hoped what she presumed was wrong. Oh, so wrong!

She listened to the ladies fussing over their dresses in the background.

"Tessa, you did a splendid job on the gowns." Solange praised, her eyes beaming.

Her assessment true. Tessa's talent and magic created the perfect multi-million dollar *Hurrikaine* wedding couture line. The purple gowns with black piping complimented each lady perfectly. The stunning, heart-stopping bride led the entourage, to the specially decorated room for the first of many photo sessions with her royal court, and later more photos expected after the ceremony.

The five women giggled as they headed for the elevator, then down eight floors to the lobby and crossed to the Empire Room. Holly's heel caught on the corner of a throw rug laid down to catch rain splatter from the guest's shoes, causing her to fall out of step and then fell behind them.

She straightened her gown and attempted to catch up, but a strong, cool hand caught her by the bent elbow and pulled her to a stop. She nervously turned braced for the worst possibility. The voice warm and familiar, the voice of her beloved.

"My Lady. You're positively the most stunning woman I've ever seen. A ravishing sight for these weary eyes that don't deserve you." Kaine turned and pulled her down another long corridor.

Too many corridors.

Sometimes they've led to Heaven other times to Hell. She relaxed as Kaine urgently wrapped her in his warm, protective arms. *Heaven*, she thought. But when she slid her arms up inside his coat, her great mood became short lived. Her worst nightmare appeared — his gun.

"Security. Don't give it another thought." He quickly dismissed.

There wasn't time to mention her terror. How the last time at Friar Manor, when he innocently gave his gun to that vicious maniac Sarah, to hold, because it defiled the stage, that bitch used it on her. Holly remembered how Sarah took the gun and placed the cold barrel next to her cheek. Almost as cold as the words, that flowed from Sarah's venomous lips.

I'll kill you, and frame Kaine for your murder.

The moment set her on edge, too chilling for the celebration she wanted to experience in Kaine's arms. No reason to tell him, but shortly she would. Soon, all the details of her foulest secrets would be out, and all would be clear between her and Kaine.

Finally.

But the question — how much danger was Kaine in? She shook, terrified because Kaine's accepted being armed with the intention of using the gun for protection against outside forces. Luka's intent the opposite, armed and waiting for any reason to shoot and murder Kaine.

Panic forced her to blurt out.

"I've decided I can't wait for a big wedding. I will go with you anywhere, my Precious One."

He leaned back in her arms to get a good look at her.

"You do remember I've asked you to marry me both at the castle and Friar Manor? And that I didn't want to wait then. I'm pleased you've agreed, and I don't have to delay our marriage any longer."

"No longer ... as soon as possible."

"Agreed. And it's important that you listen to these words. I'm sorry that I disappointed and destroyed your belief in me, in us, in London.

"These moments in love ... with you, I want to say this love is not all about the connection in bed or the fact that you're carrying our child. But when I was away from you, I missed your gentleness, your sweetness, and soft touch. I missed the sensitive lady that sat and played music with me and then wrote a wonderful song.

"I missed your kind and generous heart that believed that if you became the Lady of Briarwood, that the estate could generate large sums of money. But not to squander on useless trappings of the wealthy. But to help political prisoners, make reforms, assist in environmental causes, terminally ill people, and those treated unfairly and accused of horrendous crimes they never committed.

"See, I listened that wonderful afternoon at the castle to what an amazing woman you are. And later your heart, loving and filled with forgiveness after my tantrum.

"And I loved you more when you walked away from me.

You respected yourself, and you showed me a strength I'd never seen in a woman. And I loved you more...

"Then I decided to stay away because you deserved better than me and my fucked up demons. But I couldn't because I'd never find another you. And no matter where I went or what I did, I looked for you. In the faces of the crowds, at the arenas, on the streets, in my daydreams, and I longed for you to walk in any minute.

"But the long lonely nights? Definitely, the worst, and I missed you terribly. I'm empty without you, and I never want to be away from you again. Do you understand?"

"Yes, my Precious One, I feel exactly the same way too, and I'll never leave you again."

Kaine kissed her long and loving.

She clung to him, and if possible would never let him go.

Kaine didn't seem to mind. He behaved as if nowhere to be, no hurry.

Holly poured out her tortured heart by kissing him deeply, bound by a horrible secret she dared not tell him.

As it would surely hasten his death.

Chapter Fourteen

OVER THE EDGE

For Holly, My Lady, were the two most beautiful words in the English language. Kaine's alluring cologne surrounded her, reminding her where she belonged. He held her perfectly, within the sweet, sacred bliss of his kiss, inviting her heart and soul to melt with his, into one complete pure love.

Holly leaned back from Kaine. Her head floating so high in the clouds of ecstasy she barely heard her name called. She gazed into his luscious blue eyes, loving eyes she trusted with her life. No words passed between them. He looked handsome dressed in a black velvet coat with tails, purple silk shirt and tie, black wool slacks, and black boots. The vision of him astounding, stealing all her breath away with his magnificence's, and no one comparable.

Kaine squeezed her gloved left hand. His eyebrows knitted together with puzzlement, then beamed with pride.

"You're wearing my engagement ring."

"Yes. I belong to you, my love. Shortly, we will tell the entire world."

"You're the heart of the *Hurrikaine*, My Lady."

"Forever?" She asked innocently as her name rang out again.

"Forever, I love you," he whispered with such charm and meaning.

"I love you ... too," she vowed.

He laughed, remembering the game. "I love you three, and four times, no ... a thousand times."

She smiled happily.

Kaine kissed her briefly because her name flew down the hall with more urgency. She wanted to drown in the sweetness of his love and forget that the heinous Luka ever touched her.

Her name echoed, called again, in triplicate. She reluctantly released Kaine, turned, and hurried in the direction of the voices calling for her. She didn't dare turn around and look at her handsome Kaine because she may stop and run back into his warm, safe embrace.

"I'm sorry." She apologized catching up with the entourage.

As Holly posed for the photo session, her mind raced with all the possibilities of Sarah's involvement. It made more sense. She'd worked with Luka for years and on his private payroll. She probably had a mental map marking exactly where Luka's buried the skeletons. That's why it would be easier for him to kill her.

There were too many variables for her to control. She would need to investigate and narrow the field of possibilities and retrieve the videotape to hold as hard evidence for proof. It would surely slow Luka down should he decide to come after her, with intent to harm her.

Sarah hadn't been that smart. She'd shown Luka, her hand, and soon she would tell Kaine everything, and that action would place Kaine in immediate danger.

Holly needed to be smarter.

The time passed quickly, and the photo session ended. Holly followed the beautiful Solange, into the large ballroom next to the exclusive Canatine Room. She peeked in to see the chairs set up and a sufficient amount of flower arrangements for a coronation. Stacked along one wall, enough presents to take months to open, and years to send out thank you notes.

This taupe and gold trimmed room was where Solange would pass into marital bliss. The fairy tale setting most bride's dream. The black and purple accents reflected an appropriate elegance. And when the wedding party lined the stage that would be the second money shot sent around the world.

The first?

She didn't fool herself anymore, as a recent victim of tabloid headlines, she and Kaine, walking together, arm-in-arm down the aisle would be the scoop of the wedding.

A quiet whisper came to her ear, Emily's voice.

"Anything I can do? Go over your marks for the ceremony. You seem far away. Are you worried about when you'll see my brother?"

"A bit." That's an understatement. This wasn't the time to tell Emily about last night's private meeting with her brother. Instead, she focused on the wedding and offered.

"Thanks Emmy for walking me through since I'll lead the procession. I hope I don't make a fool of myself. It's going to be jarring enough seeing your brother and then face the world."

Since she'd missed everything the night before, she wasn't confident as she waited for her cue to begin the long walk down the aisle. However, Emily Jamison smiled as if sworn to secrecy.

The wedding march song started and close to eight o'clock when the jubilant procession moved to stroll to the altar. The groomsmen assembled in another room across the corridor, filed out, and when Luka passed her, he reached out and lovingly squeezed her elbow. She smiled back at him.

She hated him.

Then the last man exited.

Holly turned to look at her escort. There he stood, straight and tall, grateful that Solange long believed in their love when she'd paired her with Ian's best man, and he certainly was. He stood there, the most magnificent man in the entire world.

Her Kaine offered his bent elbow. She smiled graciously and tipped her head to him, telling him with her eyes that she'd love him forever, but aware that the world was watching. They proceed with extreme caution. Too much was riding on their pulling off this charade.

Kaine took her hand and squeezed it meaningfully rubbing over the engagement ring and then together they turned, paused, and faced the altar. Composed and majestic he placed her hand on his bent arm. They straightened their posture, chins held high, and they started their march, walking in unison and their hearts in harmony.

The moment arrived as intense as expected, the reunion of the Heart and the *Hurrikaine* and every eye watched them. Most gasped, others stared, but everyone looked on with interest. Holly smiled, taken aback as she passed one famous face after another. When she came to familiar smiles, Michael, and his lovely wife Catherine, she flashed them a knowing look, wondering if they would ever understand why it had to be Kaine.

Further, down the aisle sat international royalty, dignitaries, political leaders, diplomats, public officials, movie and television stars liberally sprinkled amongst the world's greatest musicians. One would have thought this occasion was a music awards banquet, not the marriage of rock music's most notable keyboardist. They traveled from around the world and from all occupations and lifestyles to celebrate Ian and Solange's marital union.

Did the jet-setting couple know every rock 'n' roll personality on the globe? And these were the privileged, attending the ceremony. Hundreds awaited their arrival in one of the three gigantic white tents erected on the back lawn of the sophisticated hotel.

The print and electronic media scrambled for exclusives for this global event. Tonight they fought each other for the perfect shot because Holly and Kaine walked together arm-in-arm. Luckily, due to the nasty weather conditions, no helicopters flew overhead. But the press skirted the grounds like insects. Yet, security was impossible to penetrate. But then that wasn't the problem. The true threat was internal!

This would be the best kick-ass wedding reception and New Year's Eve party to ring in the New Year, the tinsel town had yet to see. Holly surrendered to the beauty of the moment, and her mind abandoned the pressures of her circumstances. She looked forward to the inevitable all-star jam and then she took her place with the other bridesmaids.

She quickly glanced over to Kaine. He stood tall and magnificent. What a handsome and elegant groom he will be. Her daydreams ignited, and she imagined the nights with him, and that put a smile on her face, finally putting her at ease.

Holly's gaze drifted along the groomsmen lined up in a neat row. She hesitated when she reached Luka. His eyes pinned hers. He'd been scrutinizing her, watching her every reaction to Kaine's arrival. Though he dressed identical to Kaine, with his angel hair pulled back into a tail, the man with the blue eyes-to-die-for vanished. The emaciated shell of a heartless and soul-less creature smiled back at her. Even his once sunny smile seemed to be more of a leer.

She swallowed, calmly recognizing Luka waited to drain the core of her existence from her. She froze her facial expression refusing to register any interest in Kaine. Her stomach tossed as she flashed Luka a fabricated smile, and then carefully looked to Kaine, who moved closer, and the sight of him soothed her eyes with radiant beauty, after gazing at pure evil.

Holly looked affectionately at Solange as she repeated, "I do."

Ian exchanged his vows. Then Ian and Solange knelt at the altar holding hands. Above them, a giant screen started to descend. Kaine stepped up to a microphone, strapped on a beautiful Ovation guitar and intricately picked the strings with the opening melody to "My Lady." He sang her song as he stood to the side while the privileged guests watched clips of Solange and Ian, and their twelve-year journey to wedded bliss.

Holly never saw it. Her eyes were locked with Kaine's, his eyes locked on hers. He sang about his for her love again, and how she inspired his love for her. And everyone saw — including Luka. But she didn't notice because she stood transfixed and blinded to anyone but Kaine.

In her mind, she flashed back to their secret evening. She stood caressing the diamond on her left hand, hidden under the black satin glove.

Kaine unobtrusively returned to his place. The wedded couple rose and turned to face their families, friends, and peers. The minister looked out to the A-list crowd and proudly announced.

"I now pronounce you, Rocker and Wife."

Ian bent her back and kissed Solange senseless, amidst the roar of whistles and clapping from the delighted guests. They'd done it. "One Love" blasted out of the speakers and Ian with Solange on his arm, turned and proudly walked down the aisle. As best man, Kaine followed and came up close, oh so close to Holly.

She gently slid her hand onto his bent arm. Her hand touched the hardness of his shoulder holster for a moment as she drank in his strength.

They walked along, and Kaine bent and spoke in a loud whisper. "Listen, beautiful lady, I plan to keep my promise and announce our wedding plans at midnight."

Kaine's secret confession caused Holly to miss a step. She couldn't discuss it with him. But the warmth of his love flooded her cheerful heart.

She smiled in agreement, and those gushing feelings caused her to forget all about Luka's surprise also set for midnight.

The wedding procession reached the end of the aisle too soon for her. Holly clung to Kaine's arm. She wished she'd never have to let go, now that she'd found him again.

They stood side-by-side in the small room off to the side where everyone congregated to wait for the end of the wedding cavalcade.

After everyone had gathered, Kaine turned to give Ian a big brotherly hug.

"Ian, you asshole! You did it! I'm so proud, and you and Solange are going to have a long and happy life together."

All the while, Holly drifted in sweet memories about Kaine and their midnight secret.

Kaine! Midnight! His announcement!

It finally hit her!

Luka! Midnight! His announcement!

And then.

Tessa! Midnight!

Midnight — a few hours away.

Where *would* she be at midnight?

And where *should* she be at midnight?

The firm hand casually slide around her waist as a snake, and she closed her eyes for a split second. She braced herself because she would be looking at Luka beside her.

She took a deep breath.

She opened her eyes.

Her spirit jerked, jarred momentarily because it wasn't easy to stand in the arms of wickedness.

"Kaine. How are you mate?" Luka offered as if speaking to a comrade.

"Good Luka. Yourself?"

Luka dropped his hand from Holly's waist and stepped forward, the two men hugged each other like loving brothers. How long had they played the part?

"I see security is strict as usual," Luka pointed out acknowledging the gun.

"Yeah," Kaine confirmed. "Same with you."

He let Luka know the equivalent.

"Nothing ever changes," Luka replied casually.

They spoke as if she wasn't there just two old war buddies. No one would have guessed these men were hell-bent on destroying each other.

"Great wedding," Luka said then added, "Maybe one day soon, you'll stand next to me when Holly walks down the aisle to marry me?"

He smiled smugly as he dropped his bomb, obviously hoping to get a cheap rise out of Kaine.

It worked. Holly glanced down at Kaine's hand roll into a ball, because Luka caressed her back, casually, making it clear they were recent lovers.

She saw the hate ignite in Kaine's eyes. A thriving flame meant to extinguish Luka right there on the spot.

Kaine put on his best 'you can't bait me' expression.

But Luka already marked his territory. And to drive it home he squeezed Holly to fit the curves of his body.

She felt the gun holster.

Holly turned away from Luka, as Tessa stormed past in the opposite direction, cursing that she'd been paired with Luka, simply because she had the misfortune to be married to him.

"This is the last time I'll have anything to do with you, Luka Hunter! I swear I'd rather see you dead."

She'd have to get in a long, long line.

"What did you do to upset Tessa?" Kaine asked through his teeth.

"A little Asset business. You know how emotional she gets. We don't agree on my corporate restructuring plan."

A spiteful grin covered his face. Luka turned to Holly, pressed his lips to her cheek, and confirmed.

"Then I'll be free, Babe, to marry you."

Holly knew Luka counted on saying that rehearsed line loud enough for Kaine to hear. Holly shivered. Luka's promise took on new meaning and was horrifying.

And yes, Kaine heard. He walked stiffly beside her. She watched him wringing his hands tight the veins bulged on the back of them. And the muscles in his cheek taut from his clenched teeth didn't help her relax, he hadn't taken the threatening news well.

Her step lightens as they all headed for the Embassy Room, to start the wedding party photo session. Here she was again, sandwiched between these powerful men — the Unholy Trinity reunited. And her position too insanely tense between Kaine and Luka to take much more.

Somehow, in the melée, Kaine as best man, stood behind Holly. Luka unhappily stood trapped on the opposite side with Tessa.

Kaine slyly slipped his hands around her waist, pulled her to him, and whispered.

"No one will ever take you away from me. Especially, Luka. After our announcement, we will board the Super Star with Ian and Solange, headed for Paris.

"I have arranged everything needed for us to be married the evening of January 2, including your trousseau and wardrobe for England. Everything's settled except one detail. Do you want your parents added to the flight?"

There wasn't time, and she felt the urgency.

"Would you mind if we set another date for a wedding and reception for close family and friends?"

"No, then the course of our future is set. On January second you will become my gorgeous bride."

Holly smiled elated and erased the pictures in her mind of Luka's watchful glare, and the rapidly changing facial expressions as he became more and more upset in spite of doing his best not to let her proximity to Kaine show.

However, with each moment that passed and the longer, she leaned into Kaine, Luka's eyes grew intense, menacing, his facial expression intimidating, exposing how close he was to blowing his usual calm, English facade.

An ugly realization arrived alerting her that she would soon need to soothe Luka's ruffled feathers, after the photo shoot. She would need to be alone with Luka, for a few minutes.

Holly placed her hand over Kaine's and moved their hands down a bit out-of-sight to where she carried their baby. No matter how distasteful the idea was, she had to be alone with Luka.

She turned her thoughts to more pleasant events. In forty-eight hours, she would become Mrs. Kaine Walker.

When singled out for the best man and wedding partner photos, she gave her attention to Kaine. He whispered sweet, loving words into her ear about how incredible their honeymoon in Paris would be with the lights shimmering on the snow.

Words of his promises for a new life with her were quiet, no one else to share their private moments of elation and joy.

Chapter Fifteen

GIMME SHELTER

Holly pushed her body against the man she loved with all her heart. Kaine's alluring cologne reminded her of the wonderful times she'd spent with him the night before and in London.

All the promises Kaine whispered into her ear, of their life together at Briarwood, raising their family, traveling on vacations, and touring the world with him. But most importantly, to never, ever be apart again. It all sound idyllic. Holly moved closer to her ear, oh so close. And his warm breath tickled her and sent tiny shivers all through her.

Then Kaine quietly apologized.

"I'm going to have to disappear again for a little while. I wrote a surprise song for Solange and Ian, to perform during their reception. I'm to go on before midnight. Remember to stay close to me. I'll have our announcement to make on the stroke of midnight. Then in less than an hour we will be on our way to Paris. I love you, fiancée," Kaine pledged above a whisper as he lightly pressed his lips to kiss her ear.

Holly tensed a little. She remembered Luka's voice.

At *midnight, I have a surprise for you.*

Holly was caught in a violent crosswind between Luka and Kaine, a highly dangerous place to be.

Holly moved closer, and she nudged the holster on Kaine. She hated the reminder that he wore a gun. They both carried guns, and this created another extremely dangerous situation.

After the last photo, the wedding party scattered. They walked around stretching and mingling. Holly helped Solange tack her unending yards of the bridal train up under her waistband and were heading out when Holly spotted Kaine near the door.

Kaine turned and smiled his knowing smile as Holly casually pulled on the diamond in her ear, and he placed an acknowledging finger up to his and pulled. Kaine her handsome, elegant rock star, turned and then stepped out into the corridor. She watched Kaine about to vanish, missing him already, knowing the challenging moments she'd have to face tonight were coming.

Time to find Luka, she had something to do.

Holly paused, she smiled at her new companion.

Emily slipped her arm over Holly's, squeezing it lightly and encouraged softly.

"Holly, I've spoken to Kaine. He briefed me on what's happened to the pair of you. Oh, congratulations. My greatest dream has come true, and you have made my brother happy. He has you and the baby. I'm happy my brother has found you." A light mist filled Emily's eyes.

Holly hugged her sister-in-law to be.

"Thank you, Emmy, but please keep this to yourself. I have to draw a few boundaries with Luka before Kaine, and I announce our intentions."

Emily nodded in agreement but then suddenly, interrupted by a commotion out in the corridor.

Holly stepped out to see a woman dressed in black, a large brimmed, black hat, and black scarf draped about concealing part of her face. Sunglasses covered what she should have been able to see. Sunglasses at night? Not unusual, it was L.A.!

But this mystery woman talked to Kaine with quite a bit of animation. Kaine became visibly upset, and Holly heard his angry outbursts and indignant tone of voice, but not the actual words. Kaine jerked this woman by her arm, and a long lock of red hair rolled down her chest.

Sarah!

Holly panicked! She'd kept her threat and told him about Luka, his current plans, and with enough time, details about London. The adrenaline swept over Holly, anchoring her to the spot not knowing what to do next.

She cringed at the familiar touch of the evil slide about her, the good old serpent from Eden. She looked up to find the sinister Luka, resting himself at her side.

"Luka? I wondered where you were." She greeted with all the enthusiasm she dares muster.

"I wonder what bloody lies Sarah told Kaine to wind him up tonight?"

Luka didn't realize Holly had deciphered the double meaning in his voice as if Luka didn't have a clue to Sarah's deadly plans. Luka's smugness infuriated her, and she stifled the urge to blow him away herself. But Luka pulled her close, oh so close. She looked into the calculating eyes of a killer who planned to destroy the man she loved and steal his family.

Luka looked ugly, oh so ugly.

And she hated him.

"Look, Babe, I've got to go up to my suite for a little while. I have to ring a few contacts and have a couple of short meetings before joining the celebration. Will you go and do what you do best and mingle with the people? There may be a few future guests for the show in the crowd," his tone of voice sweet but his concern controlling. He didn't want her anywhere near anyone connected to *Hurrikaine* because that might mean she'd be nearer Kaine.

Thankfully, she'd refreshed the video camera with new tape before she'd returned downstairs. She hoped the slow recording setting on the tape would document whatever happened in his suite while she stayed away.

Holly relaxed, a bit, thankful for the reprieve hoping she would be free of Luka for a while, maybe forever.

She tried to act nonchalant and responded. "I'll miss you, but I'll go and do my best, Angel Eyes. Hot deals to finish?"

"You know me too well."

Finally, he spoke the truth.

Luka continued. "What did I ever do to deserve you? I love you Holly Hill, and I swear I'll spend my life making you happy."

He leaned in and lightly brushed her lips then allowed his passion to escalate, kissing her forcefully, deeper and deeper supposedly lovingly, purposely wrapping his body around hers for all to see.

Her stomach churned.

How much she hated him.

Holly wondered what devious plan he'd concocted this time. Whom did he plan to crush? Or, his favorite pastime — to snuff out Kaine. Luka's sweet breath assaulted Holly's senses causing her stomach to flip for another second. Luka pushed himself relentless against her rubbing with his semi-erection. How she once loved him this way. His sexual desire for her moved swiftly, and he kissed her again, more meaningfully on the mouth, squeezing her waist. Then he stopped, let go of her, turned and then exited in the opposite direction in front of the crowd and never looked back.

Thankfully!

Holly's body involuntarily shook with a sudden chill and revulsion as the invisible powers of Hell pass through her to follow Luka.

She turned to see Kaine reacting harshly to Sarah's words. And her terror careening from one end to the other in her body afraid for Kaine's life. Sarah's frightened pleas seemingly won him over and for a moment, Holly wondered how genuine was her story?

She'd threatened to frame him for her murder! But then she remembered — Sarah loved Kaine too. But then Luka loved her. Their brand of bizarre love could not be trusted. One thing she'd learned from all the suffering 'never underestimate Luka or Sarah.'

Holly moved closer.

"Kaine, please don't," Sarah begged.

Holly strained to overhear.

Kaine angrily shook Sarah's restraining hand from his coat sleeve yelling, "Don't lie you bitch! You beat her. I know everything you did to her." His voice moved, and it sounded like he stormed off in the opposite direction from her.

He'd told Sarah he knew about the events in the corridor at Friar Manor. Holly fought the compulsion to run after Kaine to warn him. The time arrived, to tell him everything. She feared for him, positive Sarah told him about Luka, how he'd set him up and then used Holly to bring him down and crush him. By doing that, she'd stupidly endangered his life.

Holly watched on, confused, not knowing what to do next.

Nicky decided. He'd hurried to Emily's side.

"Boy, I pity anyone who gets in Kaine's way. He's fucking pissed off and out for someone's blood. Someone has seriously beaten the crap out of Rah. Her face is bloody black and blue. One eye's swollen shut. She can barely speak because her lips are swollen. She whispered to Kaine what happened, I tried to overhear. But damn, it didn't make any sense. She said a few words that ignited him."

"What words?" Holly demanded.

"He kept repeating a few words — London, Luka, baby, and marriage. Mean anything to you?"

Chapter Sixteen

RIDE LIKE THE WIND

Emily clung to Nicky.

She glanced at Holly with a horrified look.

"Oh, Nicky, I'm afraid for Kaine. What did he mean by London, Luka, baby, and marriage? What does it have to do with Luka? I don't like anything that has to do with Luka and my brother."

Emily was right to be concerned that Luka was in on this. And Holly hated that she held her secret. She stood silent, holding back her tears. She understood exactly. Soon Kaine would have the entire ugly story too. Then he would fill with murderous intent aimed straight at Luka.

What should she do? Find Kaine and tell him she held important information?

Give him the videotape of Luka planning this diabolical scheme and all the behind-the-scenes pain he orchestrated with Sarah in London?

She didn't want to go to her room alone and get the video tape with the possibility of Luka nearby checking his messages. That wouldn't work because if Luka found her, he would want her body. That meant staying at the reception. She would try to keep up a good front for Solange and Ian's sake.

Nicky made the next decision for her. He offered both ladies his bent arms and invited, "Come, my lovelies, let's go to the reception. It should be time for the first dance. We'll try to make sense of this mystery there."

Distracted for the moment, Holly walked with Emily and Nicky. He leaned in close to Holly and quietly sanctioned her choice.

"Congratulations, and welcome to the family. I'm pleased that you have come to your senses. Kaine is a good man and he will treat you and your child right."

She smiled and hugged his arm affectionately.

The harried threesome passed New Year's Eve party guests from all lifestyles. The combination of upper echelon society mixed with the elite rockers milling about created a kaleidoscope of humanity one would not have expected to see at the posh New Rochelle Hotel.

They passed one ballroom after another filled with happy, carefree party crowds. Holly was preoccupied wondering where the hell Kaine went. What was he doing? More importantly, was he safe? It wouldn't do for the two highly explosive men, armed to the teeth, to run into each other somewhere all alone.

Holly, Nicky, and Emily followed the red carpet that led to a plastic canopied tunnel that ushered them to the entrance of the main reception tent. There the wedding party table's gorgeous setting waited.

They took their respective seats at the bride and groom table, and Holly noticed Solange, Kaine, Tessa, and Luka's conspicuously empty chairs while Ian sat visiting with friends and well-wishers explaining why the first dance was postponed.

Outside, the violent wind stormed, fiercely pushing against the clear plastic tent as it taunted and teased the guests, promising to break through and drench the high society and powerful elite with its commanding heavy rains.

Holly watched the tents entrance. She was also watching the lightning separate the black sky. For a split second, it dimmed the inside lights and demanding everyone's humility, proving to all below, how fierce the imposing storm's finale would be. Inside the tent hung three crystal chandeliers that shook from the traumatizing gale wind forces. The tiny glass balls crashed into each other as the thunder rolled over shaking the tent.

Holly quietly excused herself to Nicky. She looked to the other side of the tent deciding to search for Sarah and find out what she'd make known to Kaine.

Holly moved methodically, scanning the vast crowd and skirted the long buffet tables stocked with every delicacy imaginable.

What to do?

She looked out the clear plastic tent wall to observe the flashing lightning tearing up the sky, while the cruel wind continued unrelentingly, riding and snapping the walls of the clear plastic tent.

The dark intruder moved close.

Holly muttered aloud, "I've watched this fucking storm building since Tucson! I've had enough!"

She looked around, and the storm suddenly erupted into a

frightening performance, promising to devastate the reception. She screamed loudly in her mind for the storm to go away, to vanish and leave everyone she loved alone.

Her intuition ran high, and her emotions ran scared. She couldn't stand there and do nothing. But what was the best plan? She needed a plan!

She eliminated every scenario she could think of and narrow her thoughts to focus on Sarah. She was the flash point.

But where would the eruption happen?

Holly decided to move. She hoped a plan of action would follow. She methodically worked her way out of the reception's massive area, stopping every few minutes to visit with someone, hoping to keep each conversation short. Any other time it would have been a pleasure to mix with rocks elite.

But someone's life or death depended on her to locate Sarah and ascertain if she'd told Kaine everything. It took too much to work her way through the standing room only crowds. And it amazed her how many red headed women dressed in a black cocktail dress wearing a wide-brimmed hat came to the reception, leading her on one goose chase after another. Too much time passed and Holly finally decided Sarah never made it to the reception.

It struck her how irrational her thought process was ... of course, why would she with her face battered black and blue? She'd made a critical error and wasted precious time on a fool's mission. Sarah hid elsewhere in the hotel.

Then another piece of the puzzle formed.

A hand touched her shoulder startling her. She turned to

discover Emily, standing behind her. The storm caught Holly's eye outside the tent beating down, unrelenting, and at this point apparently tiring of threats. Soon, it announced, soon it would end the festivities for good.

"Holly, I can't find Kaine," Emily blurted with a panicked look, wrapped with growing terror.

At that second, a bolt of lightning pierced the sky, putting everyone on notice — it was a matter of time.

Emily's hands were shaking.

"Kaine's not rehearsing. He's not answering his suite's phone. I've paged him. He's expected to perform his wedding present for Solange and Ian before they take off on their honeymoon. I can't find him anywhere. I'm worried."

Holly tried to hide her concern and be braver than she felt. She looked at Emily and countered.

"There isn't any reason to worry. Kaine's off to a private place warming up as he always does before a performance. He'll show up when it's time."

Holly would never forgive herself for lying to Emily. She was right to be worried about her brother as worried as she was about her fiance. She needed to be unusually careful and didn't dare upset Emily with her deadly suspicions. The misleading words choked her.

Where the fuck was Kaine?

Where was Luka?

Where was Sarah?

In fact, where was Tessa?

The wrathful rainstorm twisted itself up with the unrelenting wind and produced a black imposing funnel spout. Solange suddenly approached the twosome and quietly touched Holly's forearm. Emily walked away. Her facial expression showed she tried to be as brave as Holly. But at this point, it became clear. Everyone's intuitions ran high and were worried sick.

"That's clever, what you said to Emily." Solange quietly approved. "Your quick thinking will save Emily a bit of unnecessary concern, especially in her condition."

Holly tried to smile, but she was frightened too, more frightened than she'd ever been in her life.

Solange took her elbow and moved her to the side.

"Kaine's explained your involvement with the Collin's murder trial and that if I needed help to come to you. I'm going to take you into my confidence.

"I'm a private detective investigating corporate embezzlement within the *Hurrikaine* organization. Kaine planned to tell you about this later in Europe. However, the way Luka has been behaving tonight, I need to tell you sooner. Kaine is in great danger, and because you're the one that Luka trust, we may need you to get closer to him to help keep Kaine safe."

Holly was way ahead of Solange, but she had Holly's complete attention. And she wondered if Solange heard her heart beating loudly like a hand drum?

Solange hesitated and then explained.

"There is much I need to fill in, but I don't have the time. Briefly, I've been investigating Luka and his fraudulent business practices for some time. Last summer, Kaine and I teamed up together. I'm concerned that Luka knows Kaine is onto him. It's, well, I'm not positive."

Holly looked at Solange, beautiful, unable to enjoy her

wedding reception due to the maliciousness of Luka. Reeling from Solange's confession, she decided to tell one of her own.

"You're correct about Kaine being in danger from Luka, but not from Luka knowing about Kaine investigating his business practices. I'm positive Luka doesn't suspect a thing. It's more personal," Holly quickly divulged without realizing how she gave herself away.

At this point, Holly would bet Luka remained confident. He'd never believe Kaine capable of finding out that Luka was the man behind the screen. Or, that his narcissistic confidence may be the single weakness that would bring down the great Luka Hunter's house of cards and then take him to his knees.

Holly swiftly explained to Solange. "Luka is in an extraordinarily cocky mood. His hubris makes him believe no one is on to him for any reason and would like to keep it that way."

This wasn't the time to mention Sarah and her threats to expose Luka's murderous intent because he was merely amused by her threats

Solange nodded her head in agreement.

Holly recognized Solange wondered what Holly meant by *believes no one is on to him.*

"I have my own tale to tell. And like you, I'll have to explain all that later. Look, Solange, time is important."

Solange continued. "I agree, and I need to tell you though you may not understand why this investigation is vital. Kaine bought forty-nine percent of the stock in CMT. And he speculates that Luka bought the remaining fifty-one percent of stock fraudulently with *Hurrikaine* company money.

Kaine took a big risk and put everything on the line to get

close to Luka. That's the reason he risked his sobriety and staying clean by taking the drugs, to snuggle up to Luka and be drug buddies. He'd been hoping Luka would decide to bring Kaine in on the CMT deal and give himself away. But as you've witnessed, Luka would have no part of the drugs, which did surprise Kaine. And instead of becoming confidants, events in London took a turn for the worse.

"But Kaine's breakdown in Europe, you'll understand soon why we did what we have done to you. And hopefully, you will forgive us. We tried to protect everyone. Everything's true about Kaine's depression from being separated from you. But the virus was a fabrication to make his situation look bad to take him out of the business loop as far as Luka was concerned. To make Luka believe that Kaine was removed, incapacitated and incapable of making any business transactions. We did it to throw Sarah off too since she's always worked for Luka. However, I'm afraid a showdown is coming soon."

Holly tuned out after Solange reported that Kaine knew that Luka owned the other fifty-one percent. That was something Luka counted on — that Kaine didn't know. The rest she'd understood, with her two percent, either man she married would own controlling interest in CMT. But Kaine wasn't up to speed. He didn't know that she held the all-important two percent and how Luka expected her to marry him, making the kill that much sweeter.

FUCK, and double FUCK!!!

How had this all happened?

"Solange, we have to find Kaine. Luka does know that Kaine owns the other forty–nine percent and plans to destroy him."

"What? How?"

"No time to tell. We have to find them."

"Wedding or not, I'm here to protect Kaine and find him before Luka."

"Or, the other way around and find Luka before Kaine."

Both ladies looked at each other with the knowing look of either way was dangerous.

At that moment, a man dressed as a 1920s uniformed bellhop interrupted Holly.

"Miss Hill, I've been looking everywhere for you. I have an urgent fax."

Holly took the folded piece of paper. She broke the confidential seal, opened the folded paper, and read on in horror at five printed words sent from Lucy in England. Holly folded the paper trying not to look at Solange. Her hands trembled. Solange took it from her. She read it once, then twice, and then her hands started to shake.

"No, this can't be?"

Holly was speechless.

Solange broke the terrifying moment saying, "Come on Holly we have to find Kaine and Luka. We have to stop this before something dreadful happens."

There'd been no time to move.

Suddenly, the twisting funnel spout declared it waited long enough, dropped out of the sky to blow the plastic wall covering out as if tearing tissue paper. The twisting water poured in, drenching everyone nearby and blowing away everything in its forceful path.

Silver platters stacked with hors d'oeuvres and layers of

cake flew everywhere. People clamored to move away from the airborne shrapnel of broken, jagged tableware, flatware and serving trays launched midair in every direction. The scene created constant panic and more destruction from the relentless whirling, forceful gale.

Holly turned around to look.

Solange vanished.

Holly couldn't wait any longer. She needed to find out if her worse nightmare had come true.

The crowd shoved through the tiny doorways in a panic. They searched for dryer ground. Therefore, it took longer than Holly wanted as she pushed and shoved her way to the side entrance to the hotel.

Damn, the elevators didn't work.

Of course, the storm blew down the electricity lines. Mysteriously, the backup generators to operate the hotel had not come on yet.

Holly sought the darkened stairwell. She gazed up into black nothingness. She needed to climb the eight floors to the top. She had meetings at midnight, and she couldn't be late. She thought of Solange and what a surprise she'd turned out to be.

She remembered something Kaine had told her.

Solange chose to leave Scotland Yard and become a private detective to stay with Ian. Then Ian stopped doing drugs, in fact, none of the band does anymore. I stopped four years ago. Why I am doing them, again ... it's complicated. But don't let it bother you. Very unusual things happen with the approval or knowledge of the authorities. You'd be surprised.

Yes, admittedly, she was.

And then Holly remembered what Ian told her at CMT. That he would meet up with Solange in Paris while she put the final changes on an intensive investigative report, she'd worked on for months. Solange knew all along and looked out for her since their first introduction backstage at Wembley Stadium when she found her in Luka's felonious arms.

As Holly climbed, she analyzed Solange's comment that Kaine didn't have a virus or been hidden away in rehab, as reported to throw off Sarah and Luka. But she'd missed something. A big piece of the puzzle. Why everything that was connected to *Hurrikaine* turning out to be their tour slogan — *Lost Dreams ... Lost Illusions*?

As she continued climbing she re-examining the situation. Why did Emily feed her the bogus stories about Kaine's virus? Was there any mystery or deep, dark, secret about Briarwood?

Why did Emily worry her? Had Solange and Emily trusted her so little? Yes, they were correct to believe she would tell Luka. Well, why not? The undercover work was dangerous and secretive, and they'd all watched her fall for all of Luka's lies — even defended him to all of them. They'd all tried to warn her.

Holly shook her head mystified by her own hard-headedness.

They'd all observed Luka spinning his ghastly web around her. No wonder Solange persisted after learning that Luka circled her knowing she was in imminent danger. She'd tried to coax her away from Luka with invitations to San

Francisco, but no, instead, she'd wallowed in her self-centered shame and pity. Perhaps Solange would have been able to keep her away from Luka. If she'd been able to persuade her to leave L.A., then she could have told her the truth about Kaine in Europe and then taken her to Kaine. If she'd agreed to meet with Solange, who sounded innocent, up in San Marin County, when instead, she conducted an international investigation on Luka.

And what did she do? She ran through the gates of Hell into Luka's waiting arms. No wonder Solange panicked in London, trying to get her to the Super Star with Kaine. And then unwilling to tip off Luka about the investigation, stepped aside and let her get on the CMT jet with Luka. No wonder everyone seemed disappointed she didn't catch the Super Star. They'd all been afraid for her safety.

She shouldn't blame Emily either, for protecting her brother. She was doing the same with more lies.

They'd all been in on the conspiracy because they all experienced how Luka's mind worked. Kaine, a long time co-conspirator with Luka, knew exactly who he was up against and apparently, he'd become a master at manipulating the media as well. Was that why he'd simply feigned a virus and gone home to the castle? To buy the CMT shares and let the investigation take Luka down from his powerful perch.

They'd all been afraid of Luka.

Luka's monstrous plan would have worked. The one thing Luka never factored into his plan — the blood of the *Hurrikaine*. That created the unbreakable bond between her and Kaine. One thing for sure, she needed to stop underestimating these people.

Out of breath, she finally reached the eighth floor.
She cautiously opened the door.
All quiet.
Pitch black.
Another damned corridor.
And, this time, the entrance to Hell.

Chapter Seventeen

MESSING WITH
A HURRICANE

Holly's goose bumps rode on her goose bumps.
She couldn't breathe.
She couldn't hear a sound.

The deafening storm, pounded relentlessly against the hotel's fortress, demanding to gain entrance. Her frightened mind flashed back to Friar Manor, instantly transporting her down that dimly lit corridor to Hell.

The lightning flashed through the skylight, casting pockets of light.

Why was she always in fucking corridors?

She hated the confinement — pain, too much pain. The lightning flashed again, and she closed her eyes, as she stood riveted to the floor. The thunder rolled, showing her its feelings of foreboding, remembering how lost and abandoned she'd been at Friar Manor. She recognized she stood in front of the door to Kaine's suite. She needed to move all the way down the corridor to the other side to Luka's house of horrors — a long distance to travel in the dark.

She stumbled on down the corridor.

At the same time, she heard an ear-splitting noise between

the rumble of the thunder.

Her knees weakened.

"No ... No.... That sound can't be what I think it is." She quietly affirmed under her breath.

A gun shot.

No, she reassessed, more like a crashing sound.

She moved forward.

Cautiously.

Her heart pounded louder and louder. Any minute she expected her heart to burst from her chest. And with each step she took, she became more frightened of what she would find at the end of the corridor.

"Oh, please," she muttered aloud under her breath.

"Don't let anything happen to my Kaine."

She moved and stumbled in the dark over something lying on the carpet.

She stopped in fear.

The lightning flashed again and to her horror, it illuminated why her foot tripped and what it kicked. A large clump of white bridal tuling.

In the next flash of lightning, she identified Solange's body lying in a pool of white material, splattered with crimson red liquid.

Blood.

Holly tried to muffle her scream as she quickly dropped to feel for a pulse. After a struggle, she found a faint beat.

Then another horrifying sound ran out that would compel her to leave her friend though she feared she might be bleeding to death. The loud noise differed from the other. She dreaded this sound.

Gunfire.

One shot rang out.

Apparently, her hopes had been ignored. She tried to reason in her broken mind. Another sharp sound rang out, muffled by the reckless storm. Tears of fear streamed down her cheeks. Her thoughts drifted as she inched her trembling body down the dark corridor.

She fought to keep her wits about her.

If Luka has killed Kaine, and I can't get to the hard evidence, the videotape, I will never be able to prove any of my allegations. He could kill me on the spot when I reach his suite, if, he has found out I'm in on this. No matter what, if he has killed Kaine, Luka will own CMT, the band, and if he likes, keep me as his wife and Kaine's child prisoners unable to fight his power and influence.

Her selfish thoughts persisted considering the extraordinary moments that unfolded before her. But she needed a plan when she reached the end of the corridor.

I'll be fucked with no way out, and his cold, vile hands would be touching me for the rest of my life.

Holly's stomach twisted again.

Luka planned it all out.

And so far, it worked.

She inched her way down in the dark, hoping for more lighting to brighten the corridor.

Where was everyone?

Didn't anyone hear the shot?

She wondered if Solange contacted backup.

Why was it silent, hadn't anyone, anywhere heard the shot? Of course, they're all downstairs fighting the storm, and no one climbed the stairwell to hear the shot meant to signal the end.

Holly paused within feet of Luka's suite.

The door was opened a crack. She moved closer, ever so quietly to overhear any movement.

Silent.

She didn't dare directly enter but inched her way to the edge of the room.

Darkness.

Couldn't see anything.

But then ... a light scent of him surrounded her.

Kaine arrived first, beating her there.

A long flash of lightning lit the corridor, long enough for her to catch the reflection of something on the carpet inside the doorway. She cautiously entered the suite and froze, not breathing a single breath.

Nothing happened.

Holly took a small step over to the shiny object, catching her foot on a coat lying next to it. She bent down and picked up a gold chain with a shiny pendant hanging from it. With the next flash, she saw the gold medallion she'd given to Luka for Christmas, with the clasp ripped apart.

His sentimental words came to her.

I'll never take this off.

Holly recognized it took someone strong to remove it.

The cold of the night's chill seeped into her bones. She didn't like the implications. Who ripped it off, Luka?

Dead quiet settled in the suite.

Trepidation and terror were her closest companions. She needed to peek into Luka's suite.

She stood quiet ... until the next flash of lightning. It crashed all around her setting her nerves on reserve ... then the thunder rolled shaking the building.

Did she possess the necessary courage to peek inside the room?

She waited for another flash.

She opened her eyes and saw in the fading light, a dark, faint shadow, moving quickly and cut through the darkness.

Holly threw herself back against the wall, to vanish into the black void, hoping the intruder didn't see her.

She quietly waited for the next flash. And when it tore open the sky, she stepped into the open doorway and closed her eyes for a second to steady herself.

She paused for a moment before she took a short breath preparing to face the shit of her worse nightmares.

She peered into the darkness. Her gravest fear confirmed. It unfolded in front of her eyes, and she couldn't stop the horrific images rushing into shock her fragile mind.

A cluster of strobing lightning flashed quickly and rapidly in the room. The accessory furniture demolished. Lamps and brick-a-brack tossed in disarray and shattered. She stepped and then stumbled over the destruction. There in the middle of the floor, lay the crumpled and lifeless body of her husband-to-be.

He's dead.

Holly cried out. "No. No...."

She dropped to his side and bent over him. She barely saw his face. With a flash of light, she panicked. She saw his face had been beaten badly and that if not for his dark hair and his unique scent, she would never have identified him as Kaine. Everything about his usually chiseled face was bloody and unrecognizable. His head lay in a wide pool of his own blood.

The shriek of her voice ricocheted off the walls of the suite, drowned out by the recurring thunder.

"Kaine, please, Kaine, don't leave me ... you promised," she begged.

Holly moved painstakingly slow and lifted Kaine's sweet, battered and swollen head, placing it gently on her lap. When the lightning flashed, she saw that his once beautiful face barely resembled the love of her life. She lifted her hand under his hair matted with something wet, drenched in his blood.

"Nooo, don't take him...." She wailed out-of-her-mind in agony, hoping against hope that someone heard her anguished cries.

She sat mindless, believing she was losing her Kaine. She pulled a piece of her stained dress up to wipe his bloodied face, to try to see how lethal his head wounds.

He couldn't be dead.

She sobbed again. "Don't leave me."

She whimpered as she cradled him, rocking him as if willing his spirit, his life back into his body.

Holly whispered the words to "Cold Without You" . . could he hear her? Her tears streamed, her mind cracking, too delicate to accept the catastrophic events in front of her.

She pressed his face into the fullness of her breasts. And then she snapped, suddenly pulling herself together.

Yes, he needed a doctor.

She needed help.

The immediate shock started to drain and her thoughts becoming clearer.

She pulled away, instructing herself to search for a pulse. Kaine's wound bled freely, and she leaned in close to feel his warm breath against her cheek. She found his bloody lips and tenderly placed hers on his, encouraged by the slight breath from him. She searched his neck again for a pulse. Like Solange, it was slight, but there.

He was alive!

But barely, and for how long?

The lightning flashed again.

She cautiously pulled him away from her chest to find a pillow for his head.

She saw his blood had drained all over her lap.

And there in the light of the tireless lightning, she caught the reflection of something in his hand. The hand that held the shiny black gun.

Holly froze.

Every sense on alert.

"Luka? Luka where are you, you son–of–a–bitch!" She screamed aloud. The panic suddenly lodged in her throat.

Holly waited for the lightning to flash and when it did, she quickly canvassed the room. There to her horror, across the carpet, she saw Luka.

He lay on his back.

His face as bloodied as Kaine.

The only reason she knew the body was of Luka, was due to the golden threads of his hair fanned about the carpet.

His chest, she saw it — the evil, vile blood oozing. A massive seepage of blackness stained his purple silk shirt.

Luka didn't move.

During the next flash, she made a point to notice his open eyes, yet they never moved.

Was Luka dead?

Murdered at Kaine's hand.

It was all too horrible.

Holly heard her blood-tainted screams filling the suite as the powerful wave of cold despair crashed inside her heart. The agony started in her toes, and it swept up and over her so quickly, she couldn't blink. Nausea followed and then the lightheadedness. She forgot to stay conscious, to stay with her Kaine, and keep her promise never to leave him alone.

She lost the battle to stay vigilant, and she started to drift.

Her thoughts peeled away.

Was Luka dead?

And suddenly Lucy's fax flashed in her mind.

Kaine and Luka half-brothers, they don't know.

Did Kaine kill his brother? She remembered the rest of the fax.

Edward Dunnehill father to both.

Deep inside she'd always known.

It had all been there in the eyes.

So alike, brother's eyes.

"No," she screamed aloud as the madness seeped into her mind. She couldn't accept this, would she ever be free to live and love Kaine?

"No. No...." She wailed. Her shattered voice filled the suite, for her crushed heart.

Holly drifted.

She didn't hear the tick of the clock counting down second by the second.

Nine... eight ... seven...

She passed into unconsciousness.

... Two.

... One.

Midnight.

Happy New Year!

TO BE CONTINUED...

Dear Reader,

Please do not give away the cliffhanger ending of DECEPTION.

I would appreciate it if you would please take a moment and leave a few comments about your favorite scenes wherever you purchased **DECEPTION**. It is crucial to the series to have immediate feedback while the pleasure from the story is fresh in your mind. Thank you for your valuable support.

YOU ROCK!

http://www.kewtownsend.com

KEW TOWNSEND

Affairs of the Heart ~ London

HEART (Part 1), *TEMPTATION* (Part 2)
PROMISES (Part 3), *DEVOTED* (Part 4), *BETRAYAL* (Part 5)

Affairs of the Heart ~ Hollywood

BLOOD (Part 1), *SURRENDER* (Part 2),
LIAISON (Part 3)

Forthcoming:
Affairs of the Heart ~ Briarwood

Ms. Townsend is a widow with a wonderful daughter, educator of school-age students, travel and movie buff, and writes romantic music fiction set in the 1960s-1980s rock scene in the *Affairs of the Heart Series*. She lives in sunny Southern California and loves to read under a palm tree with wave's crashing along the shoreline.

KEW's love of rock music began at a young age when she returned glass Coke bottles for change to buy 45 rpm records. Her interest moved from the music to the musicians, and living in Hollywood, interviewed the Beatles when they landed at Los Angeles International Airport. Acquiring a taste for the funny Englishmen, she began dating one of the Rolling Stones that exposed her to sex, drugs, and rock and roll. Later her memories surfaced in the *Affairs of the Heart Series* where she weaves her behind the scenes anecdotes with her long love of castles, mysteries, lightning, and thunder into a romantic suspense story. Her master's degree in Cultural Anthropology and Archaeology adds to her world travels, and flavor to her novels.

CONTACT KEW

kewtownsend.com

Leave a message, a review, and sign up for the NEWSLETTER. Be first to hear about new releases, preorders, sales, prizes, giveaways, and fun events.